CITIZENS OF NOWHERE

A Utopian Anthology

edited by
ROWAN B. FORTUNE

Published, in association with Rowan Tree Editing, by Cinnamon Press, Meirion House, Tanygrisiau, Blaenau Ffestiniog, Gwynedd, LL41 3SU

The right of the authors to be identified as the authors of this work has been asserted by them in accordance with the Copyright, Designs and Patent Act, 1988. © 2019 the authors.

ISBN 978-1-78864-094-7

British Library Cataloguing in Publication Data. A CIP record for this book can be obtained from the British Library. All rights reserved. No part of this publication may be reproduced, stored in a retrieval system, or transmitted in any form or by any means, electronic, mechanical, photocopying, recording or otherwise without the prior written permission of the publishers. This book may not be lent, hired out, resold or otherwise disposed of by way of trade in any form of binding or cover other than that in which it is published, without the prior consent of the publishers.

Designed and typeset in Garamond by Cinnamon Press. Cover design by Adam Craig.

Cinnamon Press is represented by Inpress and by the Welsh Books Council in Wales. Printed in Poland.

The publisher acknowledges the support of the Welsh Books Council.

CITIZENS OF NOWHERE
A Utopian Anthology

CONTENTS

Foreword	9
Letters From Nowhere Rowan B. Fortune	13
A Snow Goose James Perrin	32
K Jez Noond	49
The Ivory Tower Omar Sabbagh	57
Notes on Housekeeping on Earth Diana Powell	66
Separate George Lea	76
For the Sake of Seeing George Lea	93
Without Fire Ben Jacob	112
In the Stationary Cupboard Greg Michaelson	124
The Floating Market Sonya Blanck	132
By Herself Fiona Ashley	135
Three Microfictions Robin Lindsay Wilson	141
Eaters of Dreams George Lea	143
The Same Place As The Last Nina Anana	144
Biographies	180

CITIZENS OF NOWHERE

Foreword

On October 5th, 2016, British Prime Minister Theresa May delivered a speech before the Conservative Party Conference. Here, she set out a withering critique of cosmopolitanism and outlined a deep seated, parochial nationalism. The speech included an attack on those who conceive of themselves as belonging to a community that is outside of the scope of a single place:

> If you believe you are a citizen of the world, you are a citizen of nowhere. You don't understand what citizenship means.

There is a tradition in literature, one recently celebrated for its five hundredth anniversary, which has questioned far more profoundly than May the idea of what citizenship means. The stories in this anthology stem from this tradition, and represent its great and imaginative diversity. Alfred North Whitehead once wrote: 'The safest general characterization of the European philosophical tradition is that it consists of a series of footnotes to Plato.' It could be said of utopia and its subgenres that it consists of a series of footnotes to Thomas More and his book, *Utopia*. For *Utopia* the novel can be read as dystopia, as satirical anti-utopia, as allegorical fable, as political treatise. And it can be read as utopia, as an exercise of fiction that seeks to realise the outlines of a better world. One that is, as its title—u-topia, no-place—suggests, nowhere.

My hope is that the short story I added to the anthology, 'Letters From Nowhere', serves as a route into the genre. It was written to be as much a commentary on utopia as a narrative belonging to it. I do not exactly outline an ideal society, although I hint at one. What I try to achieve, instead, is an outline of the ambivalent reasons we might read and write utopias. Including the wonderful example that follows my contribution. The mid-nineteenth century mystery of Sir John Franklin's lost Arctic exploration is James Perrin's point of departure. His eco-fable, 'A Snow Goose', imagines the discovery of an ideal community; in many ways it recalls the earliest utopias, whose authors were awed by the world's scale and the possibilities of different ways of conceiving society. It is different to Jez Noond's dreamlike 'K', set in a nowhere in every sense of the word—a place, a playground, obscured by time and therefore memory. Noond's haunting story makes the reader assume the vantage of a waif with limited comprehension, truly lost in nowhere.

With 'The Ivory Tower', Omar Sabbagh adopts the perspective of Yussuf as a series of everyday encounters reveal the tensions in the man's marriage; it is a story about one of the most utopian themes, the difficulties and struggles involved in human connections and relationships, the bonds that define societies. Diana Powell's contribution is also enmeshed in everyday, recognisable concerns; she layers religious Millenarian dreams of paradise on top of a cultish, even dystopian community, and in so doing takes advantage of the short narrative form to provoke readers to consider the nature of our hopes for a better world. She exposes how such hopes can operate both as challenges to, and tools of, unjust power.

In 'Separate', George Lea conjures 'that secret and forgotten place where we played, where we conspired, where we were never children.' From this alternative and haunted topology, a parallel world, he unravels a metaphysical horror that disguises a transfiguration—Lea's work demonstrates that utopia can find fertile soil even in genres more often conceived as anti-utopian, such as horror fiction. In the accompanying 'For the Sake of Seeing', Lea develops this further, introducing two enigmatic characters as they explore the ruins of a failed utopia that hides something more transgressive and more genuinely utopian. The themes and motifs of utopia can be as shocking as any in literature.

The conceit of Ben Jacob's science fiction 'Without Fire' could operate as a meta-commentary on the utopia; it plays with ideas of authorial control and what real world concerns and anxieties motivate us to write such a work, to seek such an escape, in the first place. Likewise, 'In the Stationary Cupboard' by Greg Michaelson toys with the utopia's preoccupation with paradisal visions of life after death, in the context of a historically familiar scenario: the interment camp and the failed radicalisms of a political upheaval. Michaelson's story serves as a *memento mori*; from a place of seeming cynicism, it taps into the kernel of utopian hope and asks us to imagine a merely better world, rather than fleeing into fantasies about an altogether different one.

In Sonya Blanck's 'The Floating Market', utopia is presented to the reader in an appreciation of beauty for its own sake in the midst of desperate scarcity, all in the context of a world that is only gleamed through impressions. Here, the gorgeous, crafted prose frames a contrast between the appreciation of life and the necessity of survival. Fiona Ashley takes a different approach to subverting the genre. Her prose has the quality of a fairytale, unadorned and at a remove from its protagonist; it's a quality that fits the metaphysical drama and her ultimate, Kafkaesque twist. Ashley, like so many of the other contributors, is skilled at using the utopian prompt to comment meaningfully about what it means to be human.

As well as short stories, there are four microfictions in this collection. Three of them are by Robin Lindsay Wilson, and could aptly be called prose poems. Playing with the idea of utopia and dystopia, with elliptical moments, these pieces share with the broader genre preoccupations about time and meaning. Lea's microfiction 'Eaters of Dreams' is a strange, inverted creation myth—taking the innocence of a prelapsarian idyll and turning it on its head. The collection finishes with another short story, Nina Anana's 'The Same Place as the Last'. It assumes a traditional utopian structure, a traveller to a better future whose impressions of it serve as a commentary on the present. This story thereby brings the classic conventions of the genre to timely themes of ecological catastrophe, far right populism and the refugee crisis.

The concerns of this final story, as well as those of the whole collection, show us how the utopia as a genre can still help us to grasp and frame the challenges we face, and to do so without forcing us to retreat into a useless cynicism. For me, to be a citizen of nowhere is to be uncertainly poised between those challenges and a defiant hope that, five hundred years on from More's great contribution to literature, can rightly call itself utopian.

Letters From Nowhere
Rowan B. Fortune

Every time I pass the furniture shop down the main street in town I look inside the third window along, which contains a tableau taken from the life of some fictional person, the woman—or man, I guess—who is supposed to have configured this desk and bookshelf arrangement: its leather-bound volumes of the kind few people now own, and an old-fashioned map draped over the writing surface in all its poised clutter.

These are cues that are all chosen to suggest the life that the intended buyer should wish to live. I want another life, too; I want to be entirely somebody else and somewhere wholly other.

The nondescript cream envelopes were unstamped and unaddressed. They arrived at night, I think. Once I stayed up with Bernard dozing on my lap, flitting in and out of consciousness beside me. No letter arrived. At five in the morning, Bernard woke and barked, unusual for the old dear.

The regular mail only included a gas bill and a fifty per cent off menu items coupon for the new pizza place in town. A letter from nowhere—that was how I would come to describe them, thanks to Sayer—had not arrived through the mailbox, but when I went back upstairs one of those envelopes was waiting on my bedside table next to the tiffany lamp that Samantha bought me; that was where I would often put letters before reading them. It had materialised, as if from the ether.

The next day, the letter arrived as normal, sitting beneath the spam and official correspondence that the regular mailman dutifully delivered. It was like all the other letters from nowhere, including the one I had discovered on my bedside table. It started and ended the same as every other had.

Dear Carol,
...
Your doppelgänger from nowhere,
Carol

The sender wrote at length and created in her writings what I then thought to be an elaborate falsehood. And in her fantasy she and I were almost the same person, but whereas I inhabited a small bungalow and felt so completely alone, she inhabited this other world—the one I found so tempting, the one I craved. Most of her writings were about some fictitious nowhere that she had contrived and she traced in detail: the geography, governance, economy and architecture. She was exhaustive and meticulous and sometimes tedious.

In her fantasy the period she called 'reified human history' ended two and a half centuries ago, and this history corresponded closely enough, if not exactly, to our actual history up to around the year 1800. For over fifty days she expounded on eleventh century England, which she says is her speciality as a 'historian of the reified human.' Much of her exposition corresponded with what I read elsewhere at the time, checking her facts against those of agreed history.

After the end of rarified human history, my doppelgänger from nowhere tells me that there was a painful birth of a society rooted in the joys of what she called free labour. Humanity had been renewed and true human history begun. Humanity, she stressed with the repetitiveness of a religious mantra, had until then been alienated from itself. She gave numerous historical examples of such alienation from mass violence to awful working conditions. She had an almost monomaniacal obsession with the worst cruelties and would describe everything from the minutiae of tortures to the horrific deprivations.

> For those hanged, drawn and quartered, the victim would be bound to a wooden panel, delivered by horse to the stage for the dreadful act. They were hanged, but not allowed to die of a merciful

affixation. That way they could also have their external sexual organs removed—it was punishment reserved for men, whereas women would be merely immolated. They would also be disembowelled, beheaded and finally, literally, quartered; that is, chopped into four pieces.

Nor were her descriptions reserved for the distant past. Narrating a more contemporary war, she documented the lives of captives.

The smearing of human excrements on detainees' bodies was not an uncommon practise. The shit would be pasted across their skin, left to mangle and matt with their body hair. It was either believed that valuable military intel could be gleamed from the humiliation, or, more likely, it was a method of relieving the abusers stress and channelling their complex moral and psychological traumas.

Everything in her fantasy, an alternative to the macabre portrait of our world, began from a different footing than it would in our reality. Education, childrearing, religion, work, culture, violence, law—it required, this other Carol enlarged, a way of thinking that would be alien to me. She would stress this in terms I found utterly, exhaustingly patronising.

I did not read every letter. In the early days, when I hoped they would stop and feared their daily arrival, it was my revenge to miss a series of them. They would appear and disappear every day. They could not be kept.

Nor could they be shown. Any attempt resulted in their prompt disappearance. I would leave them somewhere definite, on a table, tacked to the fridge, within my safety box, but they would be gone all the same. I would watch them through the whole of a night, and while the thick paper would remain, it would be blank. I would look at the words through the whole of the night, but at some point I would blink and, just as surely, the words would blink out of existence too. They existed only for me. And I assumed, were a product of my febrile mind. What I came to learn later does not clarify anything. I'm writing this only because it helps me to process what has happened, not because it helps me to understand.

It was a Sunday morning and I was having difficulty with the pain. I swallowed the eighteen pills, more than half of which were medication to counteract the symptoms of the other medication, a few of which were even medication to counteract the symptoms of the medication that counteracted the symptoms of the medication. I was the old lady who swallowed the fly—I would, and still will, die.

I took the pills with the coffee the beautiful Samantha—with her pixie cut of lush brown hair and her generous smile—made me every morning. She would arrive at eight, have my coffee and porridge to me by nine and then take Bernard for a walk; the old beagle did not need a long walk. At half-ten, she would check on me one last time and leave. On Sunday mornings my son, Joseph, joined my community-obsessed daughter-in-law. The puffy rings around his eyes growing more and more, so that he reminded me of a panda bear.

This was often all the human contact I had for months. Bernard helped to keep me sane. And the letters, however disturbing, did at least break the monotony. I resisted television, radio and the Internet, those passive entertainments felt like a surrender. I could no longer manage to read a long novel. I struggled to keep up with the stories. The letters, though, felt catered to my condition.

Back then, on good days, I could still potter about outside. And in the front garden I had a bench were I sat and read the other Carol's missives when their content did not upset or bore me, and I chose to engage rather than ignore her horrors or tedious lectures.

If I had been younger—and healthier—curiosity would have propelled me sooner to research. Not only to investigate the content and claims of the correspondence, but the simple and impossible fact of magically appearing, magically disappearing, post. But I was neither. I could experience days without coherence, where thoughts would bleed into one another and the discomfort of wakefulness slid in and out of my delirious sleep. Grasping the reality of something so irreal, and doing so long enough to sustain curiosity, was a feat I only accomplished after seven months of receiving the letters.

At that time, I checked my emails about once a week on the old machine. I would wait for it to boot up, beeping, craning over my bedroom desk, against a window, looking out across the various striking blues, yellows and reds of my garden flowers. The machine would always crash onto a blue screen, what Joseph called the blue screen of death, and I would turn it off and then turn it on again and it would start-up properly, if still laboriously. Then I opened my inbox; I let the emails download for half-an-hour and returned to it to delete almost every one. Occasionally, there was a message from Joseph or the NHS or something, but most of it was for penis enlargers, Russian blondes and diet pills. And as I had no penis, had long lost interest in blondes—Georgian or otherwise—and could use more weight not less, all of it was for nought.

I had not touched the browser for over a year, having once been an obsessive addict of the online world, a hypochondriac and devourer of medical factoids, attempting to become a specialist in my own symptomatology. Charting every ache, every pain, offering my own prognoses, I competed with the pessimism of my doctors, conceiving worse and worse fates for myself. But eventually, after finding some gruesome pictures of my affliction untreated, I cured myself of my obsession and quit the web. But it was still there, my Mozilla Firefox—the delightfully named browser by which I entered this disembodied world. And there was a letter from Carol on the computer desk, one I had been reading all morning. It told me about Carol's upbringing, how she moved from family to family at will, how she had met her best friend and sometimes lover Sayer Kilby Bailly.

I typed the name into Google; if more than one Carol

Vaughan existed, why not another, but real-world, parallel for Mr. Sayer Kilby Bailly? Someone who, in that other world, had grown alongside my doppelgänger, but in this one had never met me. It demonstrates just how far gone I was to be thinking according to the logic of these letters, but I did not truly expect to find anything. And I definitely did not expect to find Dr. Sayer Kilby Bailly.

Not only did he exist, but also he had a website called Letters From Nowhere dedicated to the mysterious snail mail.

He wrote, 'These letters are far too consistent and are received by people considerably too removed to be a set of unique delusions the similarities of which are explainable in terms of cultural tropes. Perhaps some semi-mystical mechanism such as the Jungian collective unconscious provides an explanation, but whatever the reason for them, I am utterly persuaded that the majority of people who receive letters from nowhere have no shared basis for their claims.

'Nonetheless, they do share a common trait. If you have found this website because you are one of the recipients, be forewarned that you may wish to stop reading at this point. I do not wish to bring you any distress. What I am about to convey might be something you do not wish to read.

'They all, without exception, die around three and a half years after receiving their first letter and about two months after they receive their last letter.'

I stopped reading.

My first letter had arrived just over two a half years ago. If Dr. Sayer Kilby Bailly was right, I had less than a year left. And reading those words took me back half a decade to the dull, sterile white office with its slatted curtains looking out to a concrete car park, and to the long faced, greying doctor who delivered my less definite but still wounding prognosis in a dulcet tone.

I learned a long time ago to take a practical approach to time. My body aches and if I stare into the middle distance hours vanish. At first this aspect of my illness was a locus of resentment; not only was the sickness shortening my life—fifty-four and I am like an invalid—but it was robbing even the lucidity I possess for the time I have remaining. My time was being stolen from every direction: my past taken in the form of memories, my present, in my inability to hold on to waking, active life and my future by my imminent mortality.

But to resent time is just too heavy a resentment. So, gradually, I took an easier approach, happy for every daily allotment of success—just getting out of bed, a shower—and unconcerned by the inevitable, and inevitably more common, failures. When it came to time, I held the lowest possible expectations.

It was a fortnight until I returned to Dr. Sayer Kilby Bailly's website. But as I experienced that passage of moments, it could have been later the same day or after the elapsing of a whole year.

I wrote him an email outlining my situation.

He emailed back the same day, although I saw and read his email three days later:

> Dear Ms. Carol Vaughan,
>
> I hope this email finds you okay. I am so sorry to read of your illness and distress.
>
> And I am sorry if my website in any way contributed to the latter. I have the utmost belief in your letters. Your approach of keeping them secret is not rare. So much so that I wonder how many recipients never convey the important missives delivered to them and how much knowledge of this other world is consequently lost.
>
> Your scepticism is understandable, but I assure you that your letters are real. That the other Carol exists and, I strongly believe, communicates to you from benign intentions only.
>
> Please, if I could visit you anywhere, at any time of your choosing, I would deeply appreciate a chance to talk in person. Especially since you are the first

person I have met who claims that my name was mentioned in a letter. Perhaps one day this other Sayer will write to me too?
Yours sincerely,
Sayer

It was another four days before I decided to reply and a further three to fully draft and edit my response:

Dear Sayer,
Thank you for your email. As you know, I am not well, but I am prepared to accept a visit from you after my son and daughter-in-law have left from their weekly visit, at 1pm this next Sunday. Please, do not expect too much and be prepared for a very short visit.
I want to know more. Please find my details below.
Warm regards,
Carol

Small, elegant rituals still gave my life dignity. And one of my favourites—along with preparing espressos and sitting down to read—is using a letter opener. I used it on every letter from nowhere. And when Dr. Sayer Kilby Bailly's first class letter arrived with the day's letter from nowhere, I happily used it on that too—charmed that he had opted to reply offline. His letter was short:

Dear Carol,
I will arrive at the date and time given. I look forward to discussing your letters.
Yours sincerely,
Sayer

That Sunday my son's visit dragged. My eye looked to the dark grandfather clock that ticked behind Samantha and my Joseph. As usual, Joseph was quiet, staring out of the dining room window into my garden where he had played on the lawn as a boy. He was looking at the sycamore tree still growing there. Samantha talked about her work at the accountancy, weather, documentaries she liked about history or geography, the local branch of the Liberal Democrat Party and redevelopment in the town centre. Neither one of them looked at or spoke to one another.

They left at 12.30 after Samantha cleaned up and I waited another forty-seven minutes before the doorbell rang. He smiled awkwardly as I let him in, and slouched a bit too much. It took him a while to get going, but when he did the initially taciturn impression he gave was completely dispelled.

'One of those contacted, he received vivid descriptions of the cities,' continued Dr. Sayer getting close to midnight that day.

He was a short, balding man whose rotund face was framed by a closely cut red beard and large, flappy ears. He had a shy grin that belied a manic comportment when he talked of matters relating to the letters. I loved his energy.

'He did not save the writing, but was an illustrator for a major publisher. So he drew the descriptions out of his letters from nowhere. These are a rare glimpse of this other place. He gave them to me before he died; he said that nobody else would appreciate their significance. I present to you, Carol, the closest we have to photographs of this utopia.'

The beige portfolio he put down on the pale wood of my living room coffee table opened up and out spilled charcoal drawings of buildings. They were like the brutalist buildings of postwar London, except larger, more monolithic and even more ambitious in their elaborate shapes and sizes.

And there was a cleverer use of plants than I had ever seen in any real city. The monochromatic grey of the sketch at first disguised the verdant use of shrubbery, but soon I perceived that between the buildings was a thick veil of trees, and every window sported more florae so that it was as if the buildings were repositories for them rather than people. It was a city, but overgrown, a forested metropolis of strong slab monuments.

I wasn't sure what to say as he smiled from the settee, but his use of the word utopia had irked me. 'I don't know if I would call it a utopia,' I complained. 'This other Carol is insufferable and sometimes even a little frenzied. She is always condescending, especially when writing about the history of her world and in her presumptions about ours, and about me; she is a snob. If such a person is a product of utopia, perhaps I am glad not to be.'

He just kept smiling. 'I met a young man fifteen years ago, one of the first to get these letters as much as I can tell, and he told me the same thing; although, I didn't call them utopian then. Now I'm convinced. Although they are not flawless angels, their world is a kind of paradise.'

'Uh-huh,' I murmured.

'Here, look at this one,' and he shuffled through the pile of pictures to one depicting a pathway through a forest, but with buildings rising up beyond the canopy. The artist had rendered dappled light and depicted a huge crowd of people in some kind of parade, in various costumes: great, flowing dresses adorned men and women, billowing back like ship sails; elaborate hats with points and orbs and more fluttering fabrics; people in close fitting garments with patchwork designs like troupes of harlequins; masques depicting great grotesques smiling and laughing and grimacing.

'Carol always made me think of them as austere. I had in mind a society of intellectual idiots.'

'If there is one thing I have learned in my time studying the letters from nowhere, it's that utopia is a diverse place. It has an abundance of everything, a multitude of ethics and faiths and so many ways to live. Until you can interpolate more than one set of letters people always have the impression of a world taken to a single monomania. This artist believed it was a carnival utopia, a world in constant celebration. He believed that because that was his doppelgänger's life. Your Carol is, perhaps, something like an academic, maybe a member of some society of readers or perhaps a hermit contented with her studies.'

'There are hermits in utopia?'

'Apparently. This world, this other world, permits so much

more variation than ours. As far as I can tell, it reviles any attempt to impose a single template on life.'

I nodded and sipped my now cold tea. I was suspicious of all of this. I imagined coming to some vile dystopia and watching an agitprop film, like the ones doubtless made by the Nazis, describing the glorious accomplishments and perfect lives of the citizenry. I was also tired. My legs hurt and there was an uncomfortable, bloated feeling creeping from my belly to my chest, which made me irritated at having a guest present.

'I… it was…'

'Ah,' he held up his wrist, checking a clunky watch, 'I have overstayed.'

'No, not at all.'

'But I have. And I should be making my departure.' He smiled, showing off some crooked but clean teeth. 'Can I come back?'

'I…'

'You don't have to answer right now.'

'Yes, you can. Come the Sunday after next if you wish.'

Dr. Sayer Kilby Bailly is not the kind of man I would have been interested in during my youth. He was silly, excitable, a bit myopic. But weeks of enforced isolation made me happy for his attentions, even if he was mad.

When I told Samantha about him she was very interested, 'I will Google stalk him for you,' she said.

'Stalk him?'

'It's normal and it's only online, you know, to find out if people are okay. I always look them up to make sure they're not part of a cult or something.'

I agreed, reluctantly.

The Saturday before he was due to visit the second time, Samantha came to me with a deluge of information. She took Bernard off his leash and watched as he huffed over to the couch to take a long afternoon nap, snoring loudly.

'This Sayer guy part-owns an antique bookshop in London, Tomorrow's Novel. I think he runs it with his brother. They inherited the business from their father and it's famous. Been around for decades and in the same family. He has a few nieces and a dead nephew, but I don't think he's married. His Ph.D. is in biochemistry, but there's no evidence he's ever really used it. And he runs that website you mentioned. It seems kinda big. Like, there's a Facebook group, a hashtag on twitter…'

'A hashtag?'

'It's like a key word that you can use on the social network.'

'Like Facebook?'

'Yeah, kinda. Anyway, these letters from nowhere are all over. Hey, Carol, is that why you see him? Do you get these letters?'

She looked at me with her mouth clenched. She breathed in sharply.

'Yes, but please don't tell Joseph.'

Samantha laughed, but as though she hadn't meant to laugh so that it was a little violent and quickly repressed. 'Sorry, no… I mean, we don't talk much. I love the world of your son, y'know? But…'

'It's okay,' I interrupted.

As with his previous visit, Sayer was excited to talk about his favourite subject. He started, with little encouragement, by defining what makes a utopia a utopia. 'I think J.C. Davis, Karl Mannheim and Krishan Kumar provide the best definitions,' he said, as if I knew any of those people. 'They don't all agree, but we get a good idea by taking aspects of all three. First,' he held up a stubby finger, 'we need to distinguish, as Davis does, between a utopia and other ideal-worlds. For example, a utopia is not like the island of Cockaygne…'

'The island of Cockaygne?'

'Yes, it's a medieval Irish mythical place where sailors occasionally wash up. It has shops that give everything away for free and rivers and houses and streets made of infinitely replenished food. Birds will fly out of the sky and land compliantly on your fire to roast themselves for your pleasure. There's a more futuristic term for this kind of place, a post-scarcity society. A lot of modern science fictions use inexplicable technology to create the same result, but a utopia is not a world without limits. It's the world, as it exists, populated by people as they are, but it's better organised. The institutions are what is different.'

'Okay,' I said.

'Next,' Sayer held out two fingers, 'we need to understand that utopia is not about perfection. It's not perfect institutions, no more than any utopian author can expect to be able to devise such, but just better, according to someone. Mannheim gives us this part. And finally,' he held up three fingers, smiling, 'Kumar says that a literary utopia is always conveyed in a story. I think the letters from nowhere, therefore, count as utopian. In the literary sense, even if, perhaps, in some other way, they are not wholly fiction.'

'I wonder why they communicate by letter,' I mused out loud, hoping to break his flow a little.

'It is not always just letters,' he answered quickly. 'Sometimes it is emails. Especially when it involves younger people. And for one person I met, it was phone calls. Everyday a phone call, by mobile.'

'You mean, someone talked to one of these doppelgängers?'

'No, it was a pre-recorded message. And the voice was robotic, like a computer reading out text. At least according to the women who received the calls, I never heard any just as I have never seen a letter from nowhere. Nobody, as far I have been able to discover, has ever talked back to nowhere. Utopia has somehow found a way to talk to us, but it has never been the other way around.'

Sayer reminded me of my other self's way of talking, of the other Carol's sometimes endearing pomposity. I always got the impression that he loved his own voice, was intoxicated by his own words. Not in a bad way, although he could be smug, but as if he was bewitched with wonderment for any subject on which his mind rested.

He would talk on tangents on and on, his voice merging with the ambiance of my home—the dulled whoosh of cars from outside, the chirping birds from the garden, the whirr of my fan during a suffocating summer day.

There would be a lull as we drank tea, sometimes I would even drift off. 'As far as I can tell,' he would start, apropos of nothing, looking up from a pile of papers, 'they have something akin to a celebrity culture, but their celebrity culture is very niche. In fact, this quality of niche is what prevents them from being aristocratic, really. It's what holds in check their social resentment, which the evenness of their distribution would otherwise leave out of control.

'They have no household celebrities for the simple reason that they have no pervasive household culture at all. Instead, their society is a great, shifting, overlapping sea of parochialisms, adapting and altering too fast to be documented or understood holistically.

'Certain people are famous to a subset of aesthetic devotees, which will change depending on the given artist's—and they are all artists, in some sense—style of the moment. And every artist will in turn be a devotee. It is a utopia of writer's writers, painter's painters, architect's architects.' In this way he would continue and could do so, uninterrupted, for as many as five or six hours before becoming flustered, apologising, asking if I still wanted him to visit, and arranging to come by the next week or—if I felt very tired—the week after that.

Waiting for Sayer's visits had a peculiar benefit. It slowed down time. He was sometimes insufferable, but always entertaining, and because I wanted his company I felt the weight of time between each new encounter. Sayer had restored something to me, however accidentally, and I felt the same kind of gratitude to him as I had previously felt only to Samantha.

I wondered a lot about Samantha and her devotions to her husband's mother, despite her failing marriage. What obligation compelled her? I would have tried to free her of it all: myself, my son. Nobody should waste away in a loveless marriage. But I was too scared by the material implications. I selfishly wanted to keep her. And not only as a visitor, but even just as a dog walker. Seeing them—the loveless couple—sitting with each other every

Sunday morning would make me horrendously guilty, the kind of guilt you feel physically, a nausea.

I found myself asking, what would the other Carol do? No doubt sniff haughtily and accuse me of the kind of behaviour she loved to call alienated, a descriptor that she would apply equally to the crimes of hiring someone at a low wage and flaying them alive before a mass audience. Still, I wished I could ask her, ask my better self, I suppose.

The question that always hurt me most about the letters from nowhere, the questions that hurt so much it was more than ten visits before I could ask Sayer his opinion, was 'why is she not sick?' These people from nowhere only talk to us as we approach our deaths, but if Sayer is to be believed our parallel selves are never in the same condition.

The problem appeared to me as a symbol for all the inequality this nowhere represented, the simple unfairness that its existence embodied. They looked down their noses at us, but we suffered the burdens of having to live in a world that is not utopia, and furthermore of dying in a world that is not utopia.

Sayer contemplated, sipping his tea out of my bone china. 'I do not know. I have never even been able to work out why they contact people in your condition.'

'I'm dying, Sayer, there's no need for euphemisms.'

'Yes, quite,' he answered, looking at my red carpet. 'Some of the others had their own theories, would you like to know? I mean, it's speculative, I've never heard of a letter from nowhere that goes into it.'

'Yes, I'd like to know.'

'I'm not even sure how much they know about us, about the people they are corresponding with. Other than that they are talking to alternative versions of themselves, that come from a world a little like the one of their past.'

'Please, Sayer, tell me what the others thought.'

'One women, who was quite religious, a Muslim actually, thought that they were Djinn—the third sapient creations of God who exist in something like a parallel reality and have free-will. That they were mischievous, but not unkind, and that they were trying to offer pleasant stories to the dying, but they were just pretending to be our doubles, as a part of the stories. And the society they described was probably an idealised version of Djinn society. I liked that explanation.'

'I guess it makes as much sense as the letters from nowhere themselves.'

'Well, another guy, this old bloke who used to drive trucks, he took the letters more at face-value and he thought that maybe we were the dream lives of these denizens of nowhere, in some kind of shared unconscious. And that these dream selves are dying because the part of our consciousness that is separated from our true selves is waking up.'

'I'm not sure that makes sense.'

Sayer shrugged and smiled his wonky smile. 'There was one child, I met her only a few times on an oncology ward. Her parents approached me after finding my website. She said something that disturbed me. That these letter writer's were stealing our lives. That they made their wonderful world out of the life we don't get to live. They were sort of vampires to her, a world of vampires.'

'I feel a lot like that. When I read the letters, that's often how I feel.'

Sayer shrugged. 'I'm sorry, Carol.'

'It must be hard for you to do this? To go around talking to the dying all of the time? No?'

'I don't mind. I wouldn't have thought of doing it without the letters. If my nephew… well.'

A silence encroached on our conversation and threated to swallow it up.

'Did he get the letters?' I asked.

Sayer nodded, his smile this time was forced, closed mouthed. 'He was wonderful. I didn't believe him, my brother still doesn't. We don't talk about all this, what I do. But I need to know, right? And I wonder, maybe one day I will get a letter too.'

One week Sayer couldn't visit. He had to man his store. Those two weeks went slowly, not helped by some dull letters from nowhere. My utopian self could become as stuck on tangents as Sayer, and all she wanted to write about for that fortnight was her love of Parisian arcades and coffee culture.

I suspected that she lacked a clear motive for communicating and saw it more as a pen pal set-up than a means to communicate about their society. Even Bernard had abandoned me. He had been vomiting on the carpets, the smell of strong, lemony antibacterial cleaner perforated my living room. Rather than always taking Bernard back to mine, some days Samantha kept him at hers and Joseph's house, which was closer to the poor old thing's vets.

As a consequence, that one Sunday I had no visitor at all and felt a terrifying isolation, almost a vertigo.

When I did next see Sayer, it was as though he had saved up two visits worth of information to express at once. He was keener to talk about utopias than the letters. 'Their decadence reminds me a bit of... yes, E. M. Forster's 'The Machine Stops', or... or...' he clicked his fingers in annoyance, summoning the right book. 'Oh, Michael Moorcock! *Dancers at the End of Time.* But it's different, those fictional societies had no material needs and spent their time on cultural pursuits, but they weren't creative. They plagiarised and commented, like me, they were just critics and literary theorists. They were moved only by nostalgia. And in our nowhere, there's plenty of nostalgia, but all mixed up with originality. With new movements in music, paintings, writing, even new scents and fashions.

'What is it your Carol is always saying? History didn't end, right, it began. They don't see our history as history proper. They study it as kind of an anomaly, like we study pre-history. Before language, before paradise. And they believe, perhaps justifiably, that we aren't so fully human as them.'

'I hate that about them,' I interrupted.

'But they can't help it. They relate to the world and to each other on such a different plateau.'

'I hate them.' I was still angry about my long loneliness. But

Sayer's enthusiasm robbed my voice of its conviction.

He changed the subject. 'You see, a utopia doesn't just mean some ideal society, in literary terms. It's more than that, it's about better institutions.' I had heard this tangent before.

I do not believe in silver linings. Sure, a young man crippled before a war might be spared conscription, but then both conscription and disability are evils and these turns of fate do not change that essential suffering.

But Sayer, he believed in silver linings. And many of our arguments obsessed over this disagreement.

'Not everything is resolved for them,' he would be saying. 'They might have got society down, but they still die and age. They still have unrequited love. The very ingenuity of their solutions to human yearnings such as envy and despair show that these remain obstacles in their lives. Perhaps this nowhere is a utopia, but it seems to me that utopia only addresses the practical problems in a human life.

'And how depressing is it that we are still so burdened by these practical problems that for many, most, the urgent problems—the incontrovertible fact of our deaths, the enjoyment of beauty, how we form and maintain real bonds—are reduced to idle luxuries for the few to work out during their lives? They, your other Carol, are blessed, because they get to suffer in a more human way than we do.'

I rejected his argument. 'I resent what you call their decadence, but isn't it really more of a childishness than decadence? And isn't that childishness, that awe for the big problems of being human, isn't that a very hollow consolation for suffering and illness and death?'

Our arguments would always end up unresolved. But in that ellipsis, I was somehow always revived, for a time.

Five months after meeting Sayer, a fortnight after I received my last letter from the other Carol, he and I married in a quiet ceremony in my town's council building. Then, I moved to his home in London. He had a bedroom, with high ceilings and bay windows, and there he had a writing desk set up for me. The room was fitted with state of the art medical equipment beeping and buzzing around the bed.

Bernard stayed with beautiful Samantha, whom I felt would benefit from his tail wagging canine company more than I. My hope is that the poor mutt outlives me.

And it is here, in Sayer's room, that I wrote this short account. Nowadays, I keep thinking of those tableaus in the shop window, the idealised life they suggest, and how nobody in my world seems to really live a life suited to such a setting.

It's a thought that makes me resent the other Carol a little less.

A Snow Goose
James Perrin
an historical eco-fable

By turning Franklin's men into bumbling Victorian caricatures who could not learn the lessons of survival, and by portraying the Inuit themselves as savage and ignorant people who did not know what was happening in their own land, we demean both parties.

David C. Woodman,
'Inuit Accounts and the Franklin Mystery'

June, 1848. As the main body of sailors hauling the boat on its sledge across the sea ice—smoother now than where their ships were beset a hundred miles round the coast to the north—disappeared behind the island in the strait, Solomon was the first to speak, voicing all their concerns:

'I wonder if we shall see those men again on this earth, Captain?'

'Better that they head south to the Fish River,' Crozier replied, a memory of his Irish upbringing in the throaty tones. 'If another winter is to be endured, Sergeant, the hunting there is what will see those men through. We all hunt for our lives now. As to the field hospital, Mr Peddle and Mr Stanley will do what they can to restore the men to health, and Commander FitzJames and Lieutenant Irving will get them back to the ships in due course.'

His words tailed off into a forlorn silence, as though unconvinced of their own meaning. With a shake of his head he gathered himself and picked up the train of thought again: 'The stores we left they might eke out for another year. If all goes well, the men at the river can return to provision them, and once we ourselves get free of this fearful place and send out word…'

Even as he spoke, he was weighing again the decision to split his surviving men into three groups. From being a newly enlisted boy sailing out of Cork on the *Hamadryad* thirty-eight years before, he had been used to his every action being dictated by custom, order and regulation. In the year since Sir John Franklin had died—with the crews on half-rations, and the paucity of those but little augmented by what they had been able to shoot or snare on the frozen northerly coast of King William Land or amidst the ridged and tortured ice close to the ships—ingrained habits had maintained not only the discipline, but even survival itself.

Now, all was open to question. It had been five weeks since *Erebus* and *Terror* were deserted. In that time they had covered barely three miles a day, and nine more men had died. To separate was imperative if any were to live. His second in command, FitzJames, of whose mental fortitude Crozier harboured grave doubts, was too weak physically to travel much further. Despite which, he had to take overall charge at the hospital tents in Terror Bay. Crozier knew it to be a bad option, but it was the one that regulation and necessity decreed. Three of the five remaining lieutenants were among those who had succumbed to scurvy or pneumonia on the march south. Of the two still living, Irving would stay with FitzJames and Hodgson was leading the men across the ice. Splitting the party, Crozier had reasoned, and sending the strongest ahead in two groups—the larger one to establish a camp on the mainland to hunt, his own to find some way through the Arctic maze—was surely the last and only chance. If he and the six men here under his command were to survive, he knew that another model of conduct was needed, at odds with all his training. They must move light and fast through this alien land. Continually this last year, flickering through his mind had come images of the Eskimo community at Igloolik, and the winter he had spent there with Parry twenty-five years before.

Ignorant and uncultivated savages, unspeakable in their personal habits and morality, his fellow officers would always opine; though those same officers, the Irishman noted, were not above availing themselves of these 'savages' favours, be they men or women. But in Crozier, himself at a distance from established attitudes through his Irish accent and long ascent through the ranks, the memory of Eskimo friendship and resourcefulness, the recognition of what was entailed in their long survival here, was growing daily now into admiration, curiosity, respect. He remembered his excursions from Igloolik with the hunters, strove to recall the Inuk word old Aua had taught him. *Quinuituq*—that was it—deep patience! The patience of a hunter, harpoon at the ready, waiting by an *aglu*—the breathing hole of a seal; the stillness of a man as he draws his bowstring and watches the inquisitive approach of a caribou. *Quinuituq*—he mouthed the word to himself again. If there were a key to his men's survival here, surely the Eskimos and not the traditions of the Royal Navy were its custodians?

As their captain sat in silent thought, as if to dissipate the pensive mood descending upon them, his men set to loading their scant equipment, supplies and the gutta-percha Halkett boat onto the lightened sledge. Close by, a wheatear bobbed and scurried over frozen gravel. Blankey, the *Terror*'s ice-master, watched its progress, catching his captain's eye and exchanging glances.

'Come, Sergeant,' the captain spoke, 'and you, Mr Blankey, let us spy out the lie of the land.'

The marine picked up his musket, the ice-master a fowling-piece, and they followed Crozier as he climbed the brief slope. At its crest, Crozier crouched and gestured the two men urgently down. They crawled on to join him, small stones trickling into the heels of their sea boots through split and abraded seams. In front of them as they peered over, drumlins ranged north-west and south-east like shorn sheep flocking away over the mottled plain. There, a hundred paces beneath them, a first migratory caribou nuzzled at the snow, unaware of their presence.

'Watch now, Sergeant,' he whispered, 'and I guarantee it will come within twenty paces—aim for the heart.'

Slowly Crozier raised himself to his knees, head bowed and arms held high above as though he were an antlered beast. The caribou ceased browsing under the snow and turned quizzically to watch. It moved towards the men's hiding place, stopping here and there to nose at the ground, then lifting its head again and fastening a myopic gaze upon the sentinel at the hilltop. Hammer of his musket cocked, Tozer sighted down the long barrel. He remembered the contorted face of the first man he had killed— the soldier of Mehemet Ali's at Acre eight years before—remembered that then too life and death were in the balance; not slowly, as here, with disease and starvation its agents, but hovering on the point of a spear.

Barely resolving themselves into thought, his instincts turned from heat-of-the-moment action back to this watchful, silent intensity. The caribou ambled a few more paces towards them, sniffing at the air. The three men held their frozen tableau. The caribou trotted closer, halted, lifted a rear leg and turned to rub muzzle against flank as Tozer eased back the trigger, stock firm against his shoulder as the hammer struck. Powder fizzed, and the spinning ball grazed past bone to burst the animal's heart. Feet flailing, it rolled, twitched and was still, echo of the shot rolling out across the island.

'Well done, Sergeant—call the men and haul it down. We'll gralloch the beast, eat and then press on.'

Soon the caribou's belly was slit and its viscera spread out by the sledge.

'The stove, sir...' asked the sergeant. In reply, Crozier took his knife and hacked the steaming liver into seven chunks. When he'd finished he raised one to his mouth and bit off a piece, gesturing the men to follow suit. Hesitant, almost aghast, torn briefly between hunger and habit, they each picked up their portion and fell to.

'On all my voyages, I never saw an Eskimo with the scurvy. And yet we sailors always suffer. Think on that... I'm sorry, gentlemen, that we have no dinner service, nor lemon juice left to dress your meat. But nor did I ever meet the Eskimo who had use for those items, and it seems to me that we must now copy their ways. I oftentimes saw them stuff their mouths with blubber straight from white whale or seal, have tried it myself on occasion and suspect it has qualities of which we stand here sorely in need. Hot liver and raw heart for our luncheon then, friends, rare steak when we sup tonight, and we shall live to see England's shores again. A little fortitude in the matter of diet now, and Greenhithe will soon enough see you carousing along Grope Alley once more.'

And so the men dined—the marine sergeant Tozer; the whaling-fleet ice-master Blankey; seaman Manson from Whitby, who had often been north with the latter; *Terror*'s captain of the maintop Tom Farr, its coxswain John Wilson, and Osmer, the paymaster from *Erebus*. Apart from Osmer, who had been urged upon him, these were the few men still living whom he had come to trust and respect from among the assembly of Arctic tyros and those favourites of the Admiralty favourite FitzJames who had so dismayed Crozier before the expedition set sail three years ago. In Crozier's view they were smooth young gentlemen adventurers; untested in battle, without instinct for this elemental place where his own rough and hard-won knowledge surely demanded precedence—and would now take it. His responsibility as captain apart, every step away from FitzJames and the continual reproach of his polished manners and brilliant conversation assuaged bitter pangs of resentment.

Wiping the blood from cracked and blackened lips and greying beards with handfuls of snow or tattered cuffs, they loaded the carcase onto the sledge, and with a new vigour bent to the traces and hauled it back onto the ice. Behind them, a flash of white beneath the wings and the high, pealing cry of a skua caused Blankey to glance over his shoulder to where the dark bird had swooped and snatched a length of the caribou's discarded guts, trailing it across the snow. With an involuntary shudder, his cleated boot soles slipping briefly, he fell back into step.

With their captain out in front, they turned to the north-east and set a steady rhythm. The ice here in the great bay that stretched across to the mouth of the Fish River, away from the jostling and shrieking stream of pack that surged down from the Beaufort Sea, was glassy and smooth. Here and there they splashed through puddles that told of encroaching spring, or skirted round melt-holes from which, at a distance, seals watched. The sledge slid easily and the labour was light compared with hauling the boats down from Victory Point over the pressure ridges and the fractured leads. Tom Farr sang to himself as they pulled:

'*The sea, the sea, the open sea, it grew so fresh the ever-free...*'

'What's that you're groaning out, Tom?' asked Sol Tozer.

'Why, 'tis a little lament in the key of C for the delights of a life upon the land that my captain of the foretop, Mr Peglar, and I would often sing—the slip of that warm liver down my throat has put me much in mind of it.'

Before the sergeant could voice his ribald reply, Captain Crozier gestured shorewards to a shingle beach at the back of a rocky cove, sheltered from the winds.

'We shall camp there and eat well tonight, men. Come...'

The ice of the cove gleamed in morning sunlight as Tom Farr pissed against a rock wall. He looked at the dribble of thick yellow and viscous liquid that stained a shadowed drift of snow with distaste, fastened his breeches and walked down the shingle, his six companions still sleeping behind him. He gazed over the ice, studying its fractured patterns and monotone textures—gauzy, clear, opalescent—and wondered how so beautiful a substance could be so cruel, unpredictable, entrapping. How often had the same dilemma exercised him through the long months of imprisonment in the northern pack? He remembered climbing time after time to the crow's-nest to scan the horizon, always seeing the same infinite variety within monotony and emptiness. A rock round the corner of the cove shone strangely. He walked on to look at it, losing sight of the camp. Further still, he knelt by another rock to examine the contained and exquisite vigour, the brilliant colours of the lichens that had caught his attention, their names unknown to him: jewel lichen, map lichen, sunburst lichen. In a moment of vision, their seamed and flaky growths, slow-colonising, rustling out from dead and hollow centres in ages of infinite patience, were to him the true Arctic hearts. As he was absorbed, lost and insentient to all but the focus of his thought and eyes, where these and the forms of beauty he had known, whether of ocean skies or the green life of land or the secret and exotic petalled flesh between a woman's thighs, seemed entirely as one—in that moment of reverie, without uttering a cry, he was dead, his neck broken by a single blow of the stalking bear's paw as it pounced. Before his companions were awake to his absence, he was torn and chewed meat digesting in the belly of the beast as it padded silently away, back into the frozen land.

Manson, who had survived the press of 1835 in Baffin Bay, made the discovery. He saw at once what had happened, and that Farr was beyond help. Blood was spattered across the snow-patched beach where the bear had hurled his lifeless body around like a terrier with a child's toy. The seaman hastened back across the shingle to rouse and inform his captain. All six men gathered, silently building a cairn of splintered rocks over their companion's remains. When they had finished, they stood bareheaded in a cold, crystal wind as Crozier stumbled through words by now known almost by heart. At the camp they lit the spirit stove, thawed and breakfasted with scant appetite on what remained in the iron kettle of last night's feast. Would they track and kill the bear? asked Manson's old shipmate from the *Viewforth*, Blankey. But he, the captain, all of them, knew that their strength was too fragile for that, and their supplies too scant. They would press on eastwards, hoping for better hunting grounds beyond the land-bridge they believed led across to Boothia, Fury Bay, Igloolik and perhaps even home. Henceforth, muskets would be loaded and no man would venture alone out of sight. They rattled the sledge out onto the ice once more, and headed into the sun.

After four hours of hauling along a coast that ran northerly now, the men's breeches and boots soaked with splashing through meltwater shallows, they pulled out on to a rackety stone beach down which ran a freshet of good water from the thawing ground behind. As the men filled the stove and set the great black kettle to boil, Crozier took out his telescope and scanned across the bight. Fixing on a point at the back of the bay, excitedly he called the ice-master Blankey and Osmer across, handing Osmer the telescope as he arrived.

'I was told, sir, by men that have spoken with them of something the Eskimos of Baffin Bay believe. Far to the west of Igloolik and the lands of its people, they say there lives a tribe called the Netsilik. The people at Igloolik, it's said, hunt walrus, but the Netsilik are expert at catching seal—a more difficult, albeit less dangerous task.'

'Indeed, Mr Osmer, I heard a great deal about them in my time at Igloolik. It is a great mistake to assume likeness among all those we choose to term 'savages'. My friends of Igloolik, for example, were a good-natured and playful people, uxorious and happy. But I heard from them that those of Netsilik were quarrelsome, warlike and conversant with all the forms of Eskimo magic. They live in a place known as Uqsuqtuuq, which I was told translated as the place where plenty of blubber was to be had. From the look of the encampment yonder, I would say, Mr Osmer, that the soubriquet is apt.'

'That sounds like the language of Commander FitzJames,' responded the former paymaster of the *Erebus*, to Crozier's obvious displeasure, 'but if I understand your meaning aright, then this encampment surely is Uqsuqtuuk, and if their reputation is deserved, we do well to keep our weapons primed. Perhaps by means of that magic we shall ensure their cooperation?'

'I think, Mr Osmer, that a watchful diplomacy will be our first line of defence. Another haunch of caribou tonight, and tomorrow we shall introduce ourselves, I fancy. Our presence, of course, will already have been observed.'

The men hauled the sledge up to a sheltered recess in the rocks, propped loaded guns against it and made camp. Manson, with studied delicacy, peeled back hide, removed a leg from the caribou carcase and carved chunks of it into the kettle to boil whilst the others stamped cold feet and smoked short pipes. It was Osmer, standing apart from the other men and reflecting on the captain's quick rebuff, who saw the bear first. It was ambling along the ice, and it was coming in their direction. 'Sir!' he called, and gestured towards it.

Crozier assessed the situation and calmly gave out orders: 'Sergeant Tozer—move forty paces down the beach to the right. A shot from the side for its heart. Manson, on the left thirty paces; wait until it's broadside to you. Mr Osmer, Mr Blankey—behind the sledge with the fowling-pieces, and you and I, Mr Wilson, must rely on sword and pistol to give the men time to reload if it comes to that.'

The bear, as he was speaking, shambled on purposefully towards the scent of cooking meat, its low head moving from side to side, breast still faintly red from its morning feast.

'So, Mr Blankey, your friend will have his revenge,' the captain murmured, the soft shift of shingle under the bear's weight whispering as it approached. It hesitated, sensing men to the left and right, and began to lope forward. Unerringly, the marine sharpshooter's ball crashed through its ribs to the heart, and as it flailed and reared Manson's bullet pierced the belly and shattered its spine. Suddenly Blankey was vaulting the sledge and running to where the animal writhed. From ten feet he stood and delivered both barrels of heavy shot, punching through its ribs into its heart. With a last surge of strength it lunged for the ice-master, pinning him to the ground as the captain's sword sliced through its throat and Wilson's pistol discharged through its eye into the brain. A great tremor shook the vast body, coughing gouts of blood across Blankey, and with a final faint convulsion the creature died. Wrenching out his sword, the captain wiped it across the dingy yellow pelt as Tozer and Manson ran across, muskets reloaded.

'Mr Blankey...' called the captain to the crushed and blood-sodden figure under the bear.

'Aye, Captain,' came the response. 'All's well, but 'tis a heavy kind of blanket I'm lying under. I'd be grateful if you'd get me out from under here.'

Sobs of laughter greeted his words. The men took position to heave away the animal's corpse. As they did so, with unanimous instinct they glanced over at the sledge, from behind which peered the pale face of Charles Osmer.

Orpingalik arrived that night. He pushed back the pointed hood of his caribou-skin coat and called the white men, whose language he spoke, *qallunaat*. He himself, he told them, was an *angakoq*—a shaman, as they eventually came to understand. All of them would later swear that as he walked unexpectedly up the beach in midnight twilight, making them reach for the guns, he was surrounded with a shimmering and fiery light which caused the superstitious among them to believe they were encountering a ghost. But he ate the remnants of their evening meat with corporeal relish, and later withdrew a small distance to converse with Crozier, whom he addressed as Aglooka. He told of how, days earlier, hunters of his tribe had met with the other Aglooka, the weak boy in the blue coat with gold at the shoulders, who had begged seal-meat of them for himself and his three companions. He was going to die soon, Orpingalik stated, and that was his fate.

'But you, Aglooka the man, known by our people to the east, who has brought Nanuq as gift to our tribe and can hunt for yourself in this land—you will stay with us through winters to come and father children of our tribe. Though you will not see them grow into men, for like the snow geese, you will fly south before your bones whiten here. Now I will dance for you and your men, Aglooka.'

Orpingalik stepped down to a flat stretch of shingle, stilled himself and started to dance. At first he was slow, the movement studied, cautious, stealthy, deliberate, but building into a sinuous, sure, rhythmical, intertwining ecstasy, stooping, coiling, circling, pirouetting low above the beach, his expression rapt, hypnotically intense, hands always describing, floating, shaping pictures for his watchers' imaginations to grasp; of his prey, conjured up for them, immanent, there. Later the white men would talk of the presences they had seen. All around Orpingalik as he danced, the shimmering light, as though he had stepped straight from the waves, dripping phosphorescence. And as he danced, he sang this song:

> I remember Nanuq, the white one,
> The great white bear.
> With back and haunches high
> And snout in the snow he walked,
> He alone in the belief of his maleness.
> He ran towards me.
> *Unaya, Unaya!*
>
> Down I was thrown, again, again,
> Until, breathless, he lay to rest,
> Ignorant that I was his fate,
> Through whom his end would come,
> Fooled in thinking he only was male.
> I too was a man!
> *Unaya, Unaya!*

When Orpingalik had finished, he turned to Crozier: 'Aglooka, tomorrow you come with your hunters to Uqsuqtuuq. Bring your gift on the sledge for my people to see, and we will welcome you there.' With that, he walked down the beach and on to the ice, where his mercury shimmering was absorbed into the shadowy, pewter dim.

As they approached the village, dogs along the beach left off gnawing the bones of caribou and bellowed their protest. Men, women and children ran down onto the ice, calling out to Nanuq where he lay, jaws agape and snarling atop the sledge. They crowded onto the traces and heaved the load up into the village, where women using the *ulu* were scraping fat from the skins of Arctic foxes stretched on frames. A smell of boiling seal meat hung round the low stone houses. Where the ice on the sunlit side of the bay had melted, scalloped and glistening little icebergs with turquoise melt-pools on their tops floated in the sea. The women unloaded the bear and the caribou carcase and immediately started dismembering them, teasing out sinews from flesh, scraping fat from hoof and paw into bags of salmon skin, butchering the meat into ever-smaller joints, discarding only the liver of Nanuq. The six white men were ushered into the *qaggeg*— the largest dwelling in the village, where the smell of burning seal fat from the *kudlik* was overpowering and a flickering light from its moss wicks cast strange and moving shadows. Orpingalik was waiting for them there, seated on a stone bench covered with the winter hide of caribou. He gestured Crozier to walk with him to the door of the hut.

'See there, Aglooka, that far hill?'

He pointed west to where an ice mirage, a long, low chimera of a sky-hill, glimmered along the horizon.

'That is Uvayok. Before death arrived on earth a race of immortal giants lived in the north of Qiiliniq. But one summer there was no food, the walrus and the bowhead whale had disappeared, so the giants set off towards the south. South took them further from food, and so they starved. Uvayok was the largest of them. In time his body sank into the soil and the small flowers of summer grew over him until only a rib showed here and there and he became a hill. Lakes formed from the liquid that drained from his bladder. Fish swam in those lakes, and the loons called from them. Aglooka, these are our stories, the stories of the land to which you must listen now. You, and the *qallunaat* with arrow feathers on his coat...'

Orpingalik glanced and nodded to the marine sergeant.

'...you will stay here with us, hunt seal and the white whales and geese. Those other men will cross the ice before it breaks up, and will live at Taloyoak. They will kill caribou. This way, all will eat. We have lost many hunters in two springs. My daughter's husband was one of them. The women become dangerous when they have no husbands to lie with them. You white men who are strong and can hunt will take their place.'

That night, as they feasted in the *qaggeg* on seal meat, and caribou, and fermented walrus intestine that tasted within the skin like strong cheese, Crozier reflected how easily responsibility gave way to compliance in the face of greater knowledge. His fate was to have arrived here. That of those others who might still survive was now in their own hands, and he was absolved of it. After all had eaten, the women removed the blackened kettles from the *kudlik*, trimmed the wicks and recharged the trough with seal fat. Story-songs and dancing entertained them, and between the *qallunaat* and the young and widowed women glances flickered. Crozier remembered his proposal to Franklin's niece Sophie, the disdain with which it was received, the averted eyes and the sidelong quick glances as she talked later with her Aunt Jane, the scalding tinkle of their laughter. He caught a young woman's eye and thought how different was the frank and unabashed interest of her gaze. Observing them, Orpingalik whispered to him: 'Aglooka, this is Uvlunuaq, my daughter.'

Later that night, she led him back to her house, where, by the light of the *kudlik*, she took the long sticks called *tuglirak* from her hair so that it fell over her shoulders, and slipped out of her fur clothing to stand naked in front of him. Laughing, she unfastened the buttons of his frayed uniform, pulled down his breeches, helped him out of stained and ragged linen. His arms encircled her as she stood close, her breasts against his chest, feeling him rise against her. With a cracked hand, he sought out and caressed the velvet moist of her, her salt savour stinging in the split tips of his fingers: 'A man must be patient to give a woman pleasure,' she pouted, squirming away, pushing him down merrily onto the sleeping platform and tumbling with him between the heavy winter hides of caribou.

A decade passed as quickly as the bloom of fireweed in a summer season. Aglooka and the *qallunaat*-with-arrows-on-his-coat lived with their wives in Uqsuqtuuq, knowing from the other hunters that the ships had drifted away and sunk and their erstwhile companions along the northern coast were all dead. But they shunned those places where their uncovered bones lay. Children were born, as Orpingalik had promised, and when the attending women called him in to hold the squalling bundle, black-haired and red of face, Aglooka was amazed by the overpowering rush of love he felt for each one of them. Between him and Uvlunuaq too the warm laughter, the cooperation and the mutual learning flowered into understanding and a slow fondness of passion.

News came from Taloyoak, to the north across the long strait: of Wilson's uncanny expertise with a dog team ('What's a coxswain but the handler of a bunch of old sea dogs?' chuckled Aglooka, remembering a former life); of his and Blankey's journey to Fury Beach, from the cache of stores at which they had brought back muskets, and a great quantity of black powder and shot, some of which made its way back to Uqsuqtuuq in the *umiak*—the women's boat—in the summer Uvlunuaq's first-born had died.

One spring Wilson and his dogs sledged over the ice, and filled out detail for Aglooka of the rumours he had heard about Osmer's death: he had forced the wife of Ugarng whilst the latter was hunting. Before the men came back, the women had overpowered him. They had stripped him, tethered him spreadeagled to stakes of sharpened caribou bone, had cut off his genitals, put them in his mouth and left him on the slope above the summer camp in the hills for predators. The parasitic jaegers had taken out his eyes. Nanuq and his attendant daemon, the little Arctic fox, had feasted on what was left. Manson had been killed by a charging musk ox. Blankey had a wife and many children.

One year a strange *qallunaat* had come by land from the south with dogs, and the village had sold him useless things from the ships, but told him nothing of the two *qallunaat* married to women of the village who had just left for the summer camp to hunt caribou, or of those across the water.

He went away, but Aglooka knew he and his kind would be back, and Uvlunuaq knew too, as they and their children held close under the heavy hides in the dark of winter. She knew that the autumn of his life was settling on her man. In their tenth spring together, she sewed new boots for him, lined with the fur of *Nanuq*, soled with the skin of bearded seal and stitched with caribou sinews, which swelled when wet to make them waterproof.

She fashioned his coat of sealskin because she knew he would be going south, and on the morning when she heard the skeins flying high over the bay she slipped from the bed, stood so that he might see her naked for the last time and sang him this song:

I will walk with leg muscles
Strong as shin-sinew of the caribou calf.
I will walk with leg muscles
Strong as shin-sinew of the white hare.
Carefully I will turn from the dark.
I will head into the light of day.

She dressed him, tied packages of seal meat on his sledge, drums of powder and shot, a snow knife and a heavy sleeping hide. Months later, by Angikuni Lake on the Kazan River in Keewatin, Aglooka lifted the heavy fowling-piece to the hole in the canvas screen as the snow geese, black primaries stark against their brilliant white, wheeled in to land in the shallows.

The largest of them began to walk towards his hiding place over stony slopes, ground thawed billowy and summer-soft, the surface litter of stone graded into parallel or polygonal abstractions. A pair of snow buntings scurried past.

The goose paused to graze the minimal low plants that crouched beneath a dry, harsh wind—saxifrages and sedums, the roseroot and mountain avens, the cinquefoils and grass of Parnassus and fragrant shield fern, bog cotton ever-moving, the polar willow, slender-shooted, its leaves a muted, dark and unassertive green. It scratched its long neck against an old bone from the caribou herds, honeycombed and grey, mottled, with the appearance of bleached and seasoned timber, the mosses growing over it. As it did so, Aglooka's finger tensed on the trigger and squeezed.

The flash as the worn and rusting barrel split seared his eyes, a splinter of pitted steel bedded in his throat. He wrenched it free, and in doing so the razor edge cut the artery and his blood pumped out in a dying rhythm. The high tumbling calls of the geese as they hurled away across the sky, heading south, registered faintly in his fading consciousness.

His last breath rattled out in a red froth. Coyote and wolf spread his bones, the snows of winter shrouding them, and those of all the lost who would never be found.

Note: The epigraph is from David C. Woodman's fine and perceptive "Inuit Accounts and the Franklin Mystery" in Echoing Silence: Essays on Arctic Narrative, ed. John Moss, (University of Ottawa Press, 1997, p. 59). Uvlunuaq's and Orpingalik's songs are adapted from Knud Rasmussen's The People of the Polar North (1908). The Franklin Expedition to attempt to find the North West Passage set sail from Greenhithe in May 1845 in two specially strengthened bomb-ships, H.M.S. Erebus and H.M.S. Terror, carrying a combined complement of 134 officers and men, of whom five were discharged before the serious exploration began. Three more men died in the first winter of 1845-1846 and are buried at Beechey Island on the north coast of the Barrow Strait. Of the remaining 126, no survivors were ever found, though evidence and bones a-plenty were discovered and are still being discovered from the 1870s down to the present day, particularly on King William Island west of the Boothia Peninsula. Franklin's trip has become the great romantic tragedy of arctic exploration, the recent discovery of the wreck of the Erebus only adding to its allure. I was privileged to spend two months in the High Arctic as a guest of the Canadian High Commission in 1998, to report on the secession of the Inuit homeland of Nunavut from Canada's North West Territories for the Daily Telegraph. The itinerary included visits to many Franklin sites. The experience of that landscape hovering on the brink of abstraction and its indigenous people was moving and memorable. Inuit oral testimony – which informed modern opinion regards as exceptionally reliable – suggests the possibility of some such outcome as the one I describe in this story for a few survivors from among the expedition. Of the artefacts mentioned in the narrative, the National Maritime Museum at Greenwich has several on display. I have held the "fowling piece", recovered from "The Boat Place" on King William Island, that is described in the story—an experience that suggested to me the tale's conclusion.

K
Jez Noond

The black-tinted windows of the Gleaner Train obscured the world outside and the waif-boy travelled without knowledge of his route or destination. He sat opposite a Gleaner woman in the single carriage. They listened to the onboard PA. An interview with an army captain struck by lightning at a wilderness camp. Cadets discovered the unconscious officer and stretchered him home. Thunder grumbled on a loop in the pauses of the officer's tale and the boy giggled and fidgeted in his seat.

'It's better to sit still and listen,' said the woman.

The captain described his injuries, but the programme presenter interrupted. He asked the man to describe his recovery. 'I didn't understand what had happened,' the captain replied. 'I was glad to be alive.' An audience cheered as he concluded his remarks.

The boy cheered too and saw the woman smile into his face.

An interview with a diver followed. She lived on a remote island off the coast of a great land mass, somewhere far away, still diving in her old age, a whole life spent living from the sea. 'The army maintains my wetsuit,' she explained. 'There were many divers before the yield. Equipment was scarce.' The woman's voice sounded young, energetic and carefree. 'I still deep dive,' she said. 'Oysters are abundant. I don't dwell on the past.' The presenter made a joke about a mermaid and a pearl and the diver laughed courteously. An audience laughed and extended the apparent humour. 'I have a good life,' she said. 'I'm proud my daughter became a Gleaner.'

They were alone in the carriage and the Gleaner doubted the boy realised the interviews followed a script. The boy's perception of a constructed world of sounds and messages, ordered and timed for latent yet specific effect, would be minimal. The stories eased into his mind. Their mood affected him. He didn't understand their tongue.

The final package of the broadcast featured a scientist known for her work on memory and the elderly. She studied her own father under laboratory conditions. 'His ability to think forward diminished rapidly,' she said, 'and he began to fixate on the past.' Military music played under her voice. 'I tested him in the most powerful Obscura unit. It had no effect on him. It was a tricky situation. I wanted to observe him directly, but I knew he had to go in there alone.'

The train windows began to brighten, and the boy let the rhythm of trees play across his retinas, beautiful and random, blurred and hazy in the sun. The train cut through a forest, pine trees pulsed each side of the carriage. Clouds low in the sky captured his imagination, and he drifted with wild and fantastic creatures. The broadcast had finished. Pulled into his seat, he sensed the carriage as it slowed and widened his eyes towards the woman and asked her whether they were at the end of the line.

'The camp is in the forest,' she said.

She nodded through the window. He strained over his shoulder and looked for the coast. In the distance, a bank of cloud hung above the trees like smoke as though frozen in time, a single frame of some human demise. Sunlight poured into the carriage as it stopped, and the windows drained of tint. Doors slid open at their side. They inhaled hot dust.

The woman stood and pulled a rucksack from the luggage shelf above her seat. 'We're here,' she said. 'Is there any reason to wait?' She swung the canvass bag over her shoulder.

The engine at the head of the train powered-down and the carriage fell silent.

'Is broken?' the boy asked. He pulled on his duffle bag as he stood.

'No one needs it,' she said, and stepped from the carriage onto the heat of the platform.

She was at the head of a long metal ramp when the boy reached her side. They surveyed the view. The ramp led down to the edge of a sandy pine grove. The boy closed his eyes and tried to breathe, let a breeze cleanse his dirty face and shoulders, his shins. The air was still. Reflected heat scorched their advance as they took the ramp down away from the train. He looked back over his shoulder as he walked. The black engine was silent. It shimmered in the heat. End of the line. Carriage empty. Open doors. No passengers boarded or departed. The intense green of the pine behind the vehicle stabbed a blue so bright its afterimage burnt his eyes.

'Welcome to K,' the woman shouted.

He turned to see his guide on a narrow path as she disappeared through the trees. She beckoned him with a hand above her head, and he followed. He trotted to catch her, his bag banged against his spine. As he neared her, she turned and raised her palm for him to stop.

'Listen!' she said. 'No people.'

He realised he walked on fine white sand, calf muscles tighter. The soles of his feet slid in his ragged shoes. Black ants traversed the path before him. Butterflies teemed over green moss as if teased by invisible string. Bird calls filled his ears. Flocks of birds. White plumes waded against a green sea. He glimpsed them between trees. Fresh air found a way into his bony chest. He felt calm. He smiled.

A gap opened between himself and the woman. He watched her stride ahead past a wooden hut with a wide angled roof. He stopped to examine the structure further, eyes levelled with a shop counter. Ants milled over the flat surface as he peered into the rotten hut's interior. A cobweb in the frame of a porthole window pumped in the breeze like the valves of a heart. He did not understand the words and signs daubed over the slatted walls.

The boy let the sun soothe his nape and shoulders. The low whoosh of the sea, diffused through the pine, calmed him further. A tiny yellow bird swooped down onto the counter near his face, pecked up an ant and then hopped out of sight.

'Do you know what ice-cream is?'

Her voice came from nowhere.

'Not know,' he said, and turned towards her. 'What this place?' He raised a palm over his eyes.

The woman stood behind him, a silhouette against the sun.

'Playground,' she said. She held her arms out like wings. 'People once came. Plane. Train. From far. Away. The cities. Before you.' She moved closer and pointed over his shoulder into the hut. 'This is some of what's left.'

He squinted and tried to read her face 'Why still here?' he asked. He heeled the slats of the counter behind him.

'Tomb,' she said, and offered her hand. 'We should move.'

The trees broke, and she led him through dunes capped with lush grass, out onto a vast bay that stretched as far as he could see.

'K,' she announced, and traced the shape of the letter in the air for him. 'We don't use the old place names. People don't come anymore. Movement. Big travel. They ended it.'

They walked down the narrow beach to the tide's edge. There was no one to be seen.

The woman dropped her rucksack onto the sand. She pulled her t-shirt over her head and tossed it down beside the bag then ran her thumbs under the straps of her narrow top. She horned her canvass shoes off with her toes, unbuttoned her faded trousers and trod them down her legs and off with her feet. She patted her shorts as she walked the few steps into the shallows.

The boy let his duffle bag fall from his shoulder and sat on it as he watched her paddle and then wade out further. Waist-deep, she shouted to him, turned and plunged under the surface. Her feet appeared with a tail-like flick before a head reappeared seconds later, a bead stitched to a blanket of green.

She dived again. He unbuttoned his flimsy shirt and discarded it on the sand before himself. When her head reappeared, he kicked off his old shoes, the toes cut away long ago to accommodate his feet. He slid his shorts down over his narrow hips, he let the garment fall down his skinny legs to his heels and stepped from them, the sun on his naked self.

The sea was warm and shallow, delicate ridges of sand, soft rippled light, new to him as he paddled out to her. She was a dot in the distance, difficult for him to gauge. He flopped forward and pulled himself along with his fingers, kicked his feet behind. A shoal of tiny fish, beautiful and silver, flashed around him.

The woman swam further. She rose and fell on the dark power of the waves.

He panicked as he bobbed out to her on his toes, head back, chin strained. Salt water filled his nose and mouth. She disappeared beneath the surface and he paddled himself around and half-swam back to shore. An arm around his waist took him under.

He surfaced with his arms around her neck, and, for a few strokes, trailed in her wake as she swam ashore. Eyes shut, he coughed and gasped, and sensed his weight as she pulled herself from the water. She cradled him, his legs around her waist. Fear pumped in his ears and against her breast.

'Look up,' she said, 'Have you ever seen a jet? Aeroplane?'

She turned so he could see. He lifted his head from her shoulder squinted at a white line in the sky.

'If I see one, I imagine it in smothered in flames,' she said. 'An explosion.'

She let him slither form her clasp, down her legs and onto the sand next to their bags and they sat together in silence. When she reached out to touch him he raised his arm to her in defence and curled into a ball. Time passed as he listened to the waves. When he felt her hand rested on his shoulder he let it remain.

'You're clean now,' she said.

The sun set, and he listened to her talk until the voice spliced with the sea air.

He opened his eyes and sat up when she tapped his shoulder.

A small electric light glowed at the edge of the forest. A pathway. The entrance.

'Isn't that pretty,' she said.

She stood and pulled a towel from her rucksack. Turned away from him, she removed her top and shorts and dried herself.

He watched. Her nakedness was curious. He did not know his mother or father. They were sensations, capillary, body-waves that carried no image, no feature or voice, no smell of cloth or skin.

Clothes bundled in his arms, duffle bag over his shoulder, he waited for her while she dressed. She pointed to a grey structure along the shoreline, a weather-proof hut on concrete legs opposite the light at the edge of the forest.

'There,' she said, and began to walk.

The grey walls of the structure flickered into life as he approached.

Dense grids of tiny luminous beads pulsed and generated images. People. Movement. Images of people. Many people disembarked from a train, down a flight of steps towards a beach. The images played across the walls of the structure. Children swam in the sea. Parents looked on. They waved. They laid out towels and blankets and opened baskets of food. People in bathing costumes milled around and licked ice-creams. They laughed. Children played mischief. They rolled around in the sand, stood on their hands, cartwheeled through the shallow waters of the bay. A line of young women in swimsuits stood on a make-shift stage, a shiny band of fabric from each shoulder to each hip, each with a knee pushed forward, heel raised off the stage, the same precise smiles, hands tucked away.

The woman led the boy around the hut's exterior and he absorbed the images.

'Playground,' she said.

He dropped his clothes and bag and pointed at the wall of lights in front of them, at the images of a giant metal slide erected in the sea. People climbed the wide rungs of a ladder to the top of the slide, and a man dived from bottom of the chute head first into the waves.

'You'll catch a cold,' she said. 'Go inside. Go alone. Get changed.' She pointed at his duffle bag and then towards where the steps led up into the structure, the Obscura.

'What inside?' the boy asked her.

'It's an eye. Pictures inside. Upside down,' she said, and observed his frown. 'Kuleshov was correct. History must be fed directly to the brain, so the eyes do not see it. It's better that you don't understand.'

'It bad?'

'You'll get used to it.'

'What I see?'

'What happened to the playground.' She pointed to the images on wall in front of them. 'Get changed. Hurry.'

The boy opened his mouth. She raised a finger and shook her head.

She shooed him away with her hand and watched his thin naked body lit by the wall of the Obscura. He turned and climbed the steps up to door and was gone.

She was old enough to have seen her time pass. All she could do was gather the scraps and waifs from that missed harvest. She performed a role without question. She was in no hurry, but death, when it came, would be easy. Guilt would see to it.

He was inside, and walls of the Obscura dimmed to the bruise of the sky. Her eyes adjusted to the light and she waited for his return.

The sour smell of his vomit woke her. She winced but returned a sigh, empathy, as she opened her eyes. She tied his shoelaces, stood and started to walk. He followed her in the newness of the little dark uniform, the stiff shirt and neckerchief, the shorts, long socks, the shiny leather ankle boots. He slowed and watched her walk on into the darkness, towards the light and the cutting at the edge of the pine trees, her pale face a small moon when she turned back to see if he followed. She raised a hand and waved him and then turned back into the darkness.

'Now is not the time to lag,' she ordered him. Her voice boomed and echoed over the rasps of insects.

Rusted playground frames emerged from the darkness as he walked on, obeyed her command to follow, the outlines of a tractor, a space rocket, the longitudes and latitudes of a globe.

'Here,' she said, and pointed to the light. 'We wait.'

The boy slapped the metal frame of the tractor and listened to it ring like a bell across the bay.

She dropped her rucksack and forced loud shrieks of laughter from somewhere deep inside herself, as if to announce her presence. At the globe, she clasped a metal bar and pulled herself up over the surface of the construction. She waved wildly to him when she reached the top, stuck her fingers into her mouth and filled the air with a whistle that pierced his ears.

'Climb,' she demanded. 'Keep that uniform clean!'

The boy walked to the rocket frame and climbed. At its apex, he sat in the little metal seat as though ready to lift off to the stars that prickled the sky. He stared across at her with his fingers straightened at the end of his outstretched arm. He knew she was too distant, a different orbit.

'That's better,' she said, 'you're enjoying yourself.'

She untied a pouch from the frame of the globe and pocketed her payment. 'What did they sell me before?' she asked him. 'The promise of change. The same old hardship.' She grabbed a bar and rolled forward, hips against the frame, and unfurled herself inside the globe and then dropped to the sand. It was one powerful movement.

He watched as she walked back to her bag and then climbed down himself. When they were close again, she shouldered her rucksack and pointed over his shoulder.

The boy turned to see a young muscular soldier had emerged from the forest. The soldier beckoned him from beneath the lamp, a uniform the same dark tones as his own. He looked back to the Gleaner and vomited onto the sand between them. As he drew his hand across his mouth, he turned and walked towards the soldier. His back straightened, he raised a limp hand to his brow, neither salute nor mockery, the gesture of a boy who only knew a wild kind of play.

The Ivory Tower
Omar Sabbagh

'Tell me about it if it's something human.'
Robert Frost, 'Home Burial'

It was as if the wide canyon of the dark blue sky were exhaling, the weave of a navy sigh. No clouds pitted that large and wide oceanic dome; no lazy drifting puffs of gun-smoke, no ashen bubbles, globular, or pigeon-grey. But the temperature this evening was temperate, and the small whiff of a breeze whisked across their cheeks, as though imparting antique, long-buried secrets.

The returning, ambling couple were both dressed in thyme and verdigris as it happened—and that, despite the small flare-up before the outing. She had warned him, of course; but he had persisted, claiming as much right to choose his get-up as she. So that: though they looked well-knit and of-a-piece, there were pyres going off, lit and hoarse and flaming, in her mind. He, by turns, was feckless—or at least, attempting to exude the façade of such.

As they continued to stroll, strumming through and pitting the night's periwinkle air, one could feel the sour electrics between them. And just as he was about to offer a face-saving way-out for the both of them, she stopped, looked down, looked up, and huffed with terrible force, stamping her left foot as though trying to shake off a cloying demon.

'Wait,' she said, palming him her tan-colored handbag. 'Wait, will you!'

He knew the true nature of a good woman's worst nightmare. He knew that to be caught in the act of betraying trust held horrors unimaginable for the more hale-hearted dame. And he knew that his reluctance to pay like with like, his quick swallowing of pride, only made the fires in which she might be burning the more flagrant. He could almost hear the vicious, throaty roar of the flames, the doughty voice of shame; the malicious, fiercely-billowing sound as it were, of having let herself down. For all her staple love of splendor, a woman at and in her prime was never shy of a hair-shirt.

'Okay,' he said. He watched her tread softly to the curb, seat herself down and try to place the only prop to-hand between her left heel and the new oak-brown boot (one of a pair) she'd bought earlier that day. That prop, as it happened, was a smallish tampon; but this was not the time, nor the place for a smart remark.

'All's fair in love and war.' The pat phrase escaped his lips beneath his breath.

'What?'

'*What?*'

'What did you just say?'

'I said nothing.'

'No. You just said something under your breath.' She had just about managed to fit the small tampon down the back of her boot, and while getting up, pursed her lips, venomously. And when she now stamped her left foot against the ground, thrice, he didn't know whether it was merely a functional move intended to secure the prop, or a gesture of nervy frustration—with him, or at him.

The construction work outside their apartment building resumed just as they entered their flat. It was like one grand extraterrestrial hammer and tongs, pounding and clanging as though the lifeblood of nefarious aliens depended on it. Maryam hated the noise with a virulent hate, and Yusuf hated it when Maryam failed to get a good night's sleep. It wasn't just the bad temper a tossing night put her in for the rest of the following day—it was that: compounded by an extra layer of female fury occasioned by the sight of black bags under the eyes of a morning. Wounded vanity, he knew, was more plosive than your more staple, humdrum grumpy mood.

'Great,' she exclaimed. 'Just great! And how are we to sleep with this ruckus? This is impossible, impossible.'

Yusuf hummed, slow, gently. And while humming he recalled a passage in a book where the author, whom Yusuf knew to be wise, had averred that it was usually lonely people who tended to hum—habitually at least. His father was a hummer, too. But then his father had literally hundreds of friends, and each one considered him their best. Perhaps it was, then, because he, like Yusuf, was alone, bitterly alone, in the plains and tree-lined avenues of the mind? It did seem likely.

'So you enjoyed it?'

The expression on Maryam's face switched from tetchy to wondering; the transformation solicited was swift, telltale. His question served two gods: the god of 'changing-the-subject' and the god of 'getting-her-to-talk-about what she loved most.'

'The music and the performances *were* good.' She started to chew her lip, as if deliberating with herself.

For Yusuf—who like most, enjoyed a good film—a film none the less remained cordoned-off as just that: a film. But for Maryam the experience was different. When she laughed or saddened, loved or hated with or against a character, it was like the strings of her life depended on it. It wasn't just that she felt-with the movie; it was like the distance between her and the flat cinematic screen vanished, and that she was more in the thick of things than the actors themselves—who were after all only mummers and figments of, from, a projector.

The sky-loud, violently-irritating brouhaha outside halted for a few moments. Maryam now said that she wanted to try to get some sleep. Try. So Yusuf tiptoed out of the bedroom, and slouched-down to the reconnaissance of a book he happened to be re-reading for the first time in over a decade; maybe two.

'I hope the bloody-billed crane is broken! And that the tractor's wheels are now stuck in the mud. And that the shrieking Asians are gob-smacked of a sudden,' he thought to himself, in the new-forged quiet. 'For hell's a slow and succulent, undulant valley, and hell's a green and toothsome hill climbed by winning, well-loved children—compared to her acid and ire! Please God, let her sleep soundly tonight!'

Later that weekend Rami was telling them about how he'd lost and then found his wedding ring. The husband-half of a young Lebanese couple, he was telling them of his miraculous experience while they, the invited guests—all expats in Dubai—waited to be seated for dinner. His tale was a smallish marvel.

A few weeks earlier he was traipsing the monstrosity that is the Dubai Mall, a vision of wide-eyed, spilling 'excess,' and at one point his wedding ring had slipped off his finger, unbeknownst. He only realized this, he was saying, when he arrived back home later that day.

A look of mock-terror now-percolated across his face: acting-out the quick-docked fear betimes. Yusuf chuckled. So...

Fearing deep and tuneless wifely wrath, he'd phoned up the security or whatever cognate office there, responsible for such things, telling of his mishap. He asked, naturally, for them to check the 'Lost and Found.' And they duly found no ring waiting. So they called him in, needing perhaps his presence to help in the process of the search.

At this point, Rami paused, on the cusp of the marvel. He said he entered a room, well-nigh a half-mile long, with surveillance cameras wall to wall. So...

They asked him when and where he might have lost his ring. He made various calculations in his recent past's space and time, and—while peering in wonder at the sky-wide gamut of surveillance screens, still flabbergasted—was able to narrow the time and place he may have lost his ring to a workable hypothesis. So...

After trawling through hyper-detailed videos they duly found the place, the time. There was, Rami continued, a look on the foreman's face that suggested a complete dearth of doubt about the upshot of their trawling. It was as if the miles and miles of the Mall were a coin in his pocket, he said; as if space and time were compressed, for this middle-aged Emirati foreman, to a lucky nugget he might be toying with in his ochre palm. *Anyway...*

The camera in question had picked up the moving image of an Indian chap who had bent down in the area in question, picked up what looked like a ring, took a quick look around him to make sure none were watching, and slipped it neatly into his pocket. Unfortunately for this chap, as he turned to walk away, hurrying, the camera had caught a snapshot of his face. And miraculously, the foreman there, in charge of security, a man with winning oak-colored skin and deep-set amorous eyes, was able to use this image of a face to shuffle through some highly-sophisticated network of identifying images.

In short, they found the guy, and where he worked. As it happened, he wasn't employed at that Mall, but was there merely as part of some service, a delivery, to one of the retail outlets. In any case, his place of work now made known, security called up the respective company and had the man brought in. Now-caught, the latter handed over the ring, his brown face melting and glum, and replete with obsequious shame. And all this took place within a few hours of his query! So-beguiled, when asked if he'd like to press charges, Rami, being nice and a tad flummoxed by the experience, demurred.

'I was so happy and surprised (*and relieved!*)—what did it matter?'

Yusuf now joked; for here, for once, he was in his element. The central moral of the not-too-distant *Lord of the Rings*, after all, was that all that huge cinematic fanfare, all the bombast of that large adventure, all the danger and the risk, all the sadness and all the joy, centered around something as small and seemingly insignificant as a ring—a loop smaller than the size of an acorn.

Maryam, purposely, continued in her somewhat pointless chinwag with Rami's wife, paying no attention to her husband or his new-found friend.

'The Christian significance for the author, Tolkien, would have no doubt been that the absolute innocence of a newborn babe might be the living-berth of infinity, infinite wisdom, God,' he concluded, pleased, self-satisfied.

It was his nature as an inexorably-thinking man, to make some sort of inference, to elicit some kind of winnings. Again, Maryam paid no heed, making a small tinny clucking sound with her tongue, as she turned and stood up, in the manner of a slow and unfurling pirouette. Dinner was served.

*

The weekend ebbed, or scurried-away—depending on how you looked on it.

In the middle of the next working week, Yusuf found himself, snug again, hibernating at his regular. No squirrel could have asked for more comfort.

'Yes, Yes...' Yusuf now smiled. 'Yes, Yes...' He frowned, briefly befuddled. 'Yes, yes...' sibilating with obsequious glee.

That word, ever recited in duplex, that word Joyce had made the epitome of the feminine; that word, his happy hiss, was like a double-barrelled: 'Hello, hale fellow, well-met!' Mister Ricardo (*Rick to his coevals*) was the world's 'most-immediate, yes sir!' friend. Short, eminently stocky, topped by a largish square, toy-like head wagging incessantly, here was a short shrift out of the Philippines. There were, of course, many, many like him in that place, that Miracle City.

Strange thing: his studies back home had been in 'Seamanship.' Not your staple progress through or up the rungs of Hospitality Management. No, he was, by all the Fates, meant for service in some Sub-Asian Navy. And he'd told Yusuf grand tales of hardship and the winnings that capped them for those, like him, saying 'Yes, yes...'—there in that scolding place; that scalding.

Like many of his race, and his trade, he'd an incipient (and recipient) family back home, Philippine-way.

'I am a happy man,' he'd always say. And it was clear: he was. But still, a hankering hankered. Yusuf couldn't help but think, or feel, that there must surely have been some deep-bowelled negation bevelled in that slippery affirmative.

'Sir, you see, you must see...' (Again: the sibilant s's, but without hint or whiff of snake...)

The motive square of his wagging head wended downwards, inwards at him, his interlocutor, as though the flat diminutive of his weed-colored nose was attempting to penetrate the reality or the truth he wanted to impart.

Mister Ricardo was a baffling sort to encounter. He was an uncanny mix of marrow, pathos, and yet at the same time he evinced bathos as well, relief for the soul like the fresh evening air serenading that large open-spaced balcony where Yusuf was sometimes wont to have his post-graft scotch. So it was then: that he spoke of his since-discarded studies in 'Seamanship'—which Yusuf thought strange, but stupidly perhaps; because when you really thought about it, it was true that topographically and geographically Philippines was maritime!

Above all else, Mister Ricardo missed his daughter, 'Tree point pibe years, sir, she hab tree point pibe...' Her name was Alissa-Lauren, one name from he, pater, one donated by his wife, mater. She, his young daughter, 'she is my longing, sir.' Often, whether with intent or not, Mister Ricardo surprised his fellow with the odd poetic turn of phrase. For all his veneer of honed and plastic mien, there was a Homeric epic in the sorrow of being away from his daughter 'Tree point pibe years, yes sir...'

'The reason I'm here? Yes sir, yes sir... I'll tell you sir. It is simply a case of opportunity and money.' Not only was the potential to earn and save (which load was duly sent back to the maritime homeland), but the opportunity for gainful employment was much broader here, in the Miracle City. Apparently, work in the services, in hospitality, in the Philippines was rarely offered to men or women over twenty-five; Mister Ricardo was thirty-eight.

'It is because they, the young ones, are more attractib. For selling and so on. But, sir, I did not start in hospitality; with my seaman certipicate, my pirst job here was a lifeguard in the pool area of a pibe-star hotel close to the airport. Yes, yes sir.'

Then, as it turned out, the pool and recreation area was closed-down. They duly shifted Mister Ricardo to the restaurant, where he worked for the first time as a waiter. And ten years on, here he was, a Manager of a distinguished hotel's bar.

'I have one month holiday a year, to go to the Pilippines. But I miss spending both New Year and Christmas with my daughter. Yes sir, yes, I send them money ebery month; and yes sir, yes, we get by, in special because my wipe, she opened a small grocery store, and the rice sells, yes sir, it sells... But sir, my daughter—let me gib you example. The other day she burnt her thigh with the iron. And when she Skyped me that eebning—yes sir, tree point pibe, and she knows how to Skype all by herself!—I was very unhappy, I was disconsolate' (again, a lexical surprise). 'I am her pahder. And I cannot help her there, protect her. But yes sir, yes… I keep on going porward. Yes sir, yes… soon my house will be built and I will be able to return.'

A good man, ministered by a host of good angels, Yusuf now thought to himself—his short, squat, burly shoulder: a nest for the right kind of birds: larks and starlings more than rooks or cuckoos…

It was seven-thirty now; he'd been nearly two hours in that hotel bar, having stopped there on the way home from work. Yusuf knew Maryam would be waiting, with a verbal hammering on her lips. He'd promised her he'd stop his drinking—at least during the working week. He knew she was right, of course, but scotch was a temptress with more pull in the chiaroscuro of his daily routine.

So, briefly now, Yusuf excused himself from his Philippine friend, saying it was time; time to face the reckoning! He made it seem like a light-hearted quip, but it wasn't. And on his way back, traipsing the ten minutes to their flat, Yusuf pondered on what it was, precisely, that gave his wife such force and power, if not authority, in their relationship. These things, the things between men and women, had of course been going-on throughout the civilized ages, but to truly pin the gist of it with a pinpointing finger, well—that might be worth something!

Take Mister Ricardo, for example (*Rick to his friends*). He worked in a less lucrative field, was less, Yusuf ventured, attractive than himself, less intelligent or insightful, and probably less witty or funny, and so on… (*Yes*, Yusuf swiftly shrived himself: he *could* think that way.) And yet, his wife, if he'd gathered the right impression, was naught but a helpmeet. The electricity between them was no doubt the sugary kind, rather than the wasabi currently pertaining in his own, still-freshly-brewed, marriage.

Now a mere few minutes from his home, he asked himself the question:

Was there, is there, will there ever be, any mundane relationship devoid of acrid relations of power?

And his mind leapt and swerved to the thought of Nietzsche. From his earliest work onwards, life, the human condition, for Nietzsche was irretrievably 'tragic.' There was no 'positive sum' scenario. It was either 'zero,' or 'negative sum.' Yusuf parsed this to mean that in a delimited universe, when the lion lunged and bit and munched the zebra, gaining his goodly meal, the zebra, the zebra, as it were: *was fucked!* Indeed, that very morning, while seated on the toilet for his morning dump, Yusuf had been cogitating on a similar theme.

Forget the universe, he'd said to himself. Maybe it is indeed 'infinite.' But the world, the earth, *well*—we've been to the moon, we've studied and ascertained the nature of the outer atmosphere; no; the world was, undeniably, a de-limited material space. So that winning and losing were married to each other without exception, like bitter Siamese twins.

So, *yes*, perhaps life *was* tragic in its very pith and point and marrow?

Of course, Nietzsche had averred as he did, in order for us to accept and thereby transcend—create in a manner, via the foregone destruction—the predicament. Perhaps it was true that facing the lime-sour reality, beveling it rigorously inside the mind, led to more 'power.' But whether that 'power' was a kind of 'psychological' power, over oneself *and thus: only*, over one's surroundings—which was the theory and interpretation Yusuf thought best—or a more directly temporal power, well: that was a debate for the ivory tower…

Presently, he struggled, a tad tipsy, with the key in the door. It took him close to a minute to slot it aright. When, at last, he opened the door, Maryam jumped from the hidden side round the corner, and shouted: *'Boo!'*

She then burst into hysterics, bent-double and knock-kneed with laughter.

'The look on your face!'

Recovering now, Yusuf was secretly pleased.

Notes on Housekeeping on Earth
Diana Powell

Deep in the Garden of Eden, Evie is killing her mother again. Right now, it's a slow strangulation, both hands wrapped around her neck. It doesn't work, none of the ways work—the knife, the pillow, her bare hands. She always wakes too soon.

Still, she can't help these dreams that trouble her sleep, night after night, wherever she lies, inside or out. Besides, it doesn't matter. You can't kill God, can you?

A sound.

A distant thrum, hesitant at first, then stronger.

Evie stirred, disappointed. She wanted to finish her task, and silence that perfidious heart forever. She must squeeze her hands closer. She must stab again, then twist the knife; or press the pillow tighter.

But still the noise grew louder, nudging her to full wakefulness, so that, finally, she knew it came from the sky, and not the fast-fading corpse beside her.

She looked up.

An orb of burnished gold shimmered in the flaring early light. Not the sun—the sun was there, too, but in its usual place to the East. This was something else, entirely.

'There you are, Evie!' Hannah fussed towards her. 'Come in, before you catch your death!'

Death was what she wanted to catch, but couldn't, somehow. 'Look!'

One by one, the old women of the Gathering drifted onto the lawn, still dressed in their billowing organdie night-gowns, looking like errant Miss Havishams, escaped from their parlours.

'What...?'

'A congregation of cherubs!'

'An angelic host!'

'See how it directs itself at us, only us!'

'It is Him,' whispered the Divine Mother. 'We are ready. We are always ready—but...is the bed fully aired, Mary?'

Of course, they thought it was Jesus, and He was coming to join them at last.

Only Evie knew otherwise.

'No, not Jesus. An airship.'

She had learnt about it from Pathe news, in the cinema she was not allowed to visit. There had been pictures of its construction, and scenes from the airfield, in a village close by. 'I read about it in 'The Post', when I was visiting the library,' she told them. Afterwards, there was another film, showing girls her own age, dancing in a strange, syncopated style, to a matching staccato rhythm. They wore short-skirts, and Clara Bow lips, pouting around cigarettes in long, slender holders. There were other things, too, things she was not supposed to know about. The World, she guessed it was; somewhere other than the Paradise they lived in.

'It's a type of aeroplane, a giant aeroplane; like a flying hotel, with a dining room for sixty guests, and promenades with viewing platforms. They use it to take large numbers of passengers in comfort to France, or Egypt. India, even.' Her brother lived in India. She thought of India often—a place far from here.

Of course, the Gathering was saddened.

'Not Him, after all.'

'A shame...'

But... 'A sign,' the Divine Mother decided, 'most definitely a sign! How wonderful! It will not be long now!'

One by one, they returned indoors, leaving Evie alone again, to look up and wonder.

She dreamt that night of flying. Not in an airship, not at first. Instead, she flew on wings of her own. As a child, these were something she coveted. After all, why shouldn't they be hers— wasn't she the daughter of the Daughter of God? So, every now and then, she would reach behind her shoulder blades, or twist her head in the mirror, to see if wet, fledgling feathers were struggling to break free. And now, in her dream, there they were, strong and powerful, taking her up, up in the air, high above the Garden. But then her mother appeared, beckoning, calling to her. 'Evie, Evie, come back; you must come back!' And the cry, and the momentary loss of concentration made the wings stutter, then crumple, so that she fell down, down, towards the earth. Slowly, at first, then pell-mell, faster, so that she would surely crash and break to smithereens, like the fragile planes of the war, killing her older brother. But no... there she was, caught by her mother's waiting arms. 'You see, Evie, how I always save you, how you are always mine! Forever!'

She supposed the dream meant something, just as those other dreams did. She had read of Dr Freud in 'The Strand'—another forbidden entertainment. And she guessed it was a sin, for hadn't her mother announced that dreams could be sinful? She would have to confess to it—an offering, perhaps, in exchange for those she dare not own to.

And, sure enough, the Divine Mother was waiting when she went downstairs.

'Is there something you want to tell me, my dear?'

And yes, it was a sin.

'Yet angels fly, and they are the servants of the Lord.'

'And Jesus rose up through the air to Heaven, to be beside His Father.' But she kept these protests locked tight in her head, along with her real misdemeanours, and accepted her punishment silently.

It was an easy enough penance, after all—'housework for the Lord, Evie, since it will not be long now!'

And it was something she was used to, and did routinely, for the maids came, then went again, afraid that the madness would trap them. And the women, who thought they were so fastidious, were ageing fast, or else were lost in Godly contemplation. So, each night, she trailed around after their forgetfulness, closing a door here, a tap there, switching off the light that lingered in the cellar.

And, each morning, she would find their old-age littered around the place afresh. Silver hairs woven into the antimacassar, so that she must unpick each one, as if it was a poorly-worked thread in the lace. Brightly coloured sweet-wrappers, folded tightly and pushed deep in the folds of sofas and armchairs, hidden like stolen treasure.

And always, there were the smells—talc, parma violets, peppermints, and something else she thought must be secreted in the deepest crevices of their bodies, beyond the reach of their clawing hands, beyond her reach.

She would work, today, to banish them. She knew what to do. It was written down in her mother's neat script, presented to her on her twenty-first birthday, when it was decided she should live in the New Jerusalem, beside her. Chosen. 'Happy Birthday, Evie!'

'Take a jar of beeswax and mix with oil of lavender collected from the Garden of Eden. Mix hard. Polish the table until you can see your face in it.'

So she rubbed and rubbed and rubbed, until she could see her ghostly shadow, with its dead eyes, and pleading mouth — features that didn't belong, that she didn't want to see.

They were there again, when she cleaned the windows.

'For glass, take some vinegar, then finish with newspaper, until it shrieks like a poorly played violin!'

And in the mirror, that they had debated endlessly. 'Will Jesus want a mirror? Will He know what one is?'

What Jesus wanted was the heart of it all. 'Will Jesus like what He finds here?' she must ask, as she went from room to room, making her lists, ticking her boxes. 'Will He be happy to live amongst us in Paradise, forever?'

And then, last of all, she fetched the broom, and brushed Satan through the door, along with the detritus of the old women.

'See, Evie, how you have purified your soul, as you have cleansed the house! God is merciful!'

'Yes, mamma. Of course, mamma. Thank you, always, dearest mother.'

*

And when she had finished, it was time for God to speak—as He did every day, as the clock struck five, directing His thoughts through His Daughter.

And just as Evie had expected, there were new rules on account of the airship.

The Gathering most certainly was not to fly.

'We are women and men, given arms and legs; we are creatures of the Earth. That is where we belong. That is where we must remain.'

Mr Darwin had said that man came out of the water, yet another thought that could not be voiced aloud, for the Divine Mother had condemned Darwin as blasphemy.

And boats, too, were forbidden, so England, this island, was where they must stay.

'Satan is everywhere. Better to stay close at hand. I myself will not venture more than seventy-seven steps from our community. God asks you to do the same.'

How would Evie reach India now? Or France, where she had been once-upon-a-time in some other life. Or... anywhere?

'And why should we seek to leave here, anyway, when 'here' is Paradise on earth, and where He is coming to?'

It was strange how God's views always matched her mother's. How it had always been that way.

The airship returned a few days later.

Evie spied it from the attic window, where she slept above Jesus's bedroom.

If she could see it, perhaps those inside could also see her.

Perhaps they were looking down, even now, from the promenade window, at the little town, with its nice, straight rows of streets, lined with its solid, presentable red brick houses, and neat squares of tidy gardens, until their eyes were drawn by the confusion of Paradise, and its Garden, and on to a tiny figure waving frantically from its perilous perch.

Well, she was used to being watched. It was what the Gathering did, what she herself did, too—watch each other, then tell.

'The pie-dish that Lizzy washed is still crusted with pastry on the outside,' she had told the Divine Mother only yesterday.

'Elsa is looking unkempt again,' she had reported last week. 'Her hat is inappropriate, and the hem of her skirt is stained with mud.'

Well, it was true, and it must be told, so that Elsa could be admonished, and Improve. That was what they must do—*Improve*. That was the way to live forever, if that was what you wanted…

They must be vigilant of each other at all times. So it was right, last night, to crouch in the shadows of the landing and make no sound, and watch as James skulked outside Henry's door, waiting for Edward to emerge, so that he could take his place. And when Edward had gone, it was right to move closer to the door, and listen to the sounds that came from within— sounds she did not fully understand, so that when she finally withdrew to her room, her dreams were not of killing her mother, nor of flying, but of being inside Henry's chamber, in Henry's bed, where he touched her in places that were forbidden… where she found herself touching, when she awoke—if, indeed, she had ever been sleeping.

Another confession. She was not supposed to think about the touch of a man on her body. Such things were not for her, not for any of the women. And she must tell about Henry and the others, too… whatever it was they were doing.

Another punishment, greater now. No visits to town for a week. 'It is obvious you are vulnerable, my dear. There is more need for Improving.'

There must be more housekeeping.

At least she was allowed into the Garden, for there was work to be done there, tidying it away for the winter. Leaves to be brushed up and gathered, fallen twigs and boughs to be taken to the wood-store.

The wood-store was where the serpent lived. She had discovered it last summer, when an unseasonably chilly night had led them to call for a fire. It had crawled past her, whispering. And that same night, the dreams of killing her mother had begun; before, it was simply her own life she wanted to finish.

In the first Garden of Eden, the serpent had been the cause of the Fall, leading Eve into temptation. But she wasn't Eve; she was Evie. Perhaps the creature sought out the weakest victim for its spell, for it was surely the serpent who had caused the dreams, making them grow from silent suffocation with an embroidered cushion, worked by her own fair hand, to a teaspoon of rat poison slipped day after day into a carefully prepared porcelain cup of lemon tea, to a knife—silver, shining brightly—pushed into the heart, and twisted and twisted and tearing and tearing, and stabbing again and again and again... the kind of dream she had been having when the airship first arrived. But how could this happen, when her mother had decreed *their* Garden to be Paradise regained—a place to defeat the Fall, and Satan with it? An idyll where everyone was doomed to be saved?

James appeared beside her; he had been punished, too. When James first joined the Gathering, she had been foolish enough to imagine he looked at her. James was young, whereas Henry and Edward, who had joined earlier, were twice her age. Most of the young men had died in the war, blown to bits on Flanders Fields, or in those paper aeroplanes, along with her brother. Otherwise, there would have surely been one for her, a husband, keeping her away from here, saving her from being saved. Yet Mamma told her she was lucky—to be untouched was the chosen path, the best way, to live amongst them. 'It is easier to Improve that way; it is easier to be Immortal.'

And then James had arrived. She placed herself before him, whenever she could, but, always, he would simply excuse himself, and hurry away. She had sat next to him at dinner, or made sure they must squeeze together in the doorway. Yet he paid her no more attention than the others—the old women, the men, the servants, even. (He worshipped her mother, of course, but that was only to be expected. Everyone worshipped her mother; she was God on Earth, after all.)

But then, one day, in the Garden, she had seen him sitting with Henry, who placed his hand on James's arm, talking and edging closer all the time, talking and moving his hand to James's knee. And then they rose from the arbour, and went back into the house, so she followed them upstairs. That was the first time she had stood in the shadows outside Henry's door, that was the first time she had heard those strange noises, that stirred her deep inside.

'Henry is leaving,' James told her, now. 'The Divine Mother has ordered it.'

Because of her tales, she presumed.

'And Edward, too.'

James was being allowed to stay, on account of his youth and innocence.

'I am blessed,' he said.

They carried on, stacking the wood, that had fallen from the apple tree, along with its rotting fruit.

She told him about the serpent.

He poked about with a stick.

'It is a slow-worm,' he said. 'Completely harmless. There is nothing but good here.' She should have known, her mother was right. Only the fruit was corrupt—the fruit... and Henry. And Edward.

'Where will Henry go?'

'To America, he and Edward, both, to seek a new life away from us—poor things.'

'Poor things'—who had been allowed to cross the water; who were allowed to go far away. They had done wrong, yet this was how they were punished.

'Was there no way of Improving them?' she asked.

'Sadly, the Divine Mother thought their sins were too great, that they were beyond saving.'

'What did they do?' she asked him.

James moved closer to the wood-pile, and pushed the stick in further.

'They... I believe... they came to know each other too well.'

She put her hand on his arm. 'We know each other well, James, don't we?'

James hurried away from her, praying under his breath.

She looked down at the slow-worm. It was a serpent,

whatever James said. Why else would she have such wicked thoughts?

When she was allowed back into the town, she sashayed through the door of Woolworth's, bold as brass... on through the stands of beads and baubles in rainbow colours; the glass towers of sherbet fizzes and lemon-drops; the rows of smiling dolls, and pocket-money toys—led to the make-up counter by the stifling odour of cheap perfume. The sales-assistants gawped at her, and whispered to each other through painted lips, behind their gaudy nails. 'Can I help you, love?' one asked, giggling. 'India,' she remembered. 'Flying,' she thought. She turned, and fled.

'Boots is far more respectable. Always use Boots,' she remembered her mother saying. She should have listened to her mother. Boots stocked make-up, too.

Back home, she tipped her wares onto her dressing-table, wondering what she had scooped up from the counter and somehow bought. She opened them one by one, unscrewing this jar, dipping her finger inside, sniffing that pot. The clasp of the compact defeated her at first, but she liked the swivel of the lipsticks, once she had got the hang of it, though their names puzzled her. She opened 'Chinese Red' and slid it along her lips, then pursed them together. 'Who is that?' she wondered, looking in the mirror, where a flesh and blood reflection gazed back at her. And when she had finished with the powder, the rouge, the eye-shadow, the mascara, she slipped off her clothes, one by one, until she made her way, naked, to James's room.

'Oh, Evie, poor Evie! You are ill!'

It seemed she had not sinned at all; she was simply unwell, and must stay in a bed beside her mother, day after day, week after week. 'How can I be ill, here?' she wanted to ask. How could anyone be ill, with the daughter of God ruling over them, blessing the water they drank with her breath, pronouncing them Immortal?

'Dear Lord, keep Evie safe from harm, make her clean again,

willing and ready to live forever and ever. Amen.'

The world without end…

Evie walked down the road, step after step, on the squares of the pavement, following the straight lines of the walls, down the nice streets towards the muddled edge of the town. She looked at her map again. She had stolen it from the library, just after she had come from the forbidden cinema, where she had seen that the airship would be leaving soon for Egypt; Egypt was a boat trip away from India and her brother. She was tired now, and it was further than she thought. Her bag was heavy, the day surprisingly warm. But still Evie walked on. Today was the day of departure. She had no plan, beyond getting to the airfield, where the film had said there would be crowds of people, milling around the ship, waiting to wave it away. Who would notice her amongst them? Who would notice if one more slipped aboard?

Dusk fell over the Garden of Eden, whilst somewhere over Beauvais, the golden airship fell to earth.

'How sad!' said Elsa.

'So many lives lost,' announced Mary.

'But perhaps… '

'…unfortunate, yes, but a lesson, perhaps, to us all,' said the Divine Mother. 'You see, how right I was, to forbid flight!'

'Where's Evie?'

'We must tell Evie. She will be upset, she seemed to have an attachment to it.'

'Too much so, perhaps.'

'…the cause of her illness, perhaps.'

'Where is Evie?'

'Evie?'

Separate
George Lea

I find her there, where the grass is still scorched, the ground still stained. Where else but on the edge, between worlds? The state she wears so like that last day: pale, freckled skin, fiery hair, a sun dress of white cotton whipping about her slender legs in a faintly chill breeze. I don't know what sky she sees; an example of what the Old Gardeners considered perversity, once: the reality she experiences augmented, altered by intention and design. Depending on mood, she might see an expanse of blameless Summer blue or knots of Autumnal tumors, threatening rain. Perhaps stars wheeling and super novas exploding, suns and planets cycling in a celestial dance through the naked cosmos. A condition of perpetually flocking birds or swarming butterflies, of silver snow or dead broadcast static.

The world is theirs; their painting, their poetry.

As it could be ours, if only...

'Shut up.'

That voice, whispering through the drowned sermons of those whose memories I've done all in my power to murder. The one I forgot, until recently, when I met him there, in that secret and forgotten place where we played, where we conspired, where we were never children.

The interface is old, certainly by the standards of the world beyond the walls, but more than sufficient for us. No child of the Old Garden born without it, though the means of its encoding was long lost. Not that we needed to know; the anatomy as much a part of us as our eyes and lips, our bones and hearts: part of being *human*.

How closed off from one another must they have been, those old people who murdered the world? How alone in their skulls?

An intimacy we indulged perhaps too much, certainly

according to Hunter and the rest of the Gardeners. A perversity, whose demands only escalated as we grew:

I feel her blossom in my hand, my own palm and fingers flowering in response. A circuit made of our clasped flesh, our intertwined nerves, known since our earliest years, like waking from a dream, meeting again and for the first time, not in the waking word, the Old Garden, but...

Here, in one of many playgrounds that we dreamed for ourselves, in the timeless, boundless space between our skulls.

A place we've dreamed and elaborated since we were children, since its first, rudimentary scrawls, an infantile crayon drawing growing in sophistication with every passing day, every fresh stroke.

I stumbled, laughing, as I always did. That sense of impetus, of tumbling, almost enough to carry me off my feet, down the hill's flank, gambolling through its silver grasses, its purple and yellow flowers, churning up the scarlet soil beneath.

She arrested my fall, holding my hand, drawing me back. Laughing still, though there was a chill in the air that day, a new bitterness like coming frost.

An expanse that shamed the Old Garden, rolling plains of hills and small forests, coruscated by deep valleys, vast enough to contain towns and villages, to house civilisations. Silver rivers and dark trees, a sky that shifted between imminent storms and deep, deep dusk. Creatures grazed and danced amongst the plains, things we'd read about or whose names and natures were encoded in our DNA, knowledge of them flowering from birth, dreamed of in the womb: dogs and dinosaurs, crows and cattle. Things beyond anything evolution ever produced, that could only be found in the pages of fantastical fiction or surrealist paintings.

From here, atop the hill that was its first site, the original coalescence, we saw it all: watched its denizens about their hunts and grazings, their games and mating rituals.

Others trespassed here, sometimes: echoes of them all around us, ghosts that shimmered on the air in all colours, some flocking to us, pleading for us to grant them access, others fleeing, dissolving into the pale light.

We denied any and all. So much wiser, here, always: so much more than we were or could ever be, in the Old Garden.

Ours. Not a *garden*; nothing so planned or proscribed, no fences to bound it, no design or pattern to tame it. And we were different there, too, though we always forgot upon parting, the memory fading like a dream after unwanted awakening (some fault in the coding? Some deliberate failsafe, for the sake of sanity?).

No longer recognisable as who we were, as children within the walls.

The woman that held my hand was tall and willowy, her bared skin dusted with pulverised stars, her hair long, flowing as though caught in oceanic currents. Her eyes ablaze, a third in her forehead burning brightest.

Somehow I saw myself through those eyes, as she smiled at me, as embers rose from between her teeth.

A living statue, an idealisation of lithe and sculpted musculature, of acrobatic grace. Dark skinned where hers was pale, every inch of my flesh crawling with animated tattoos, that told stories of what we'd done here, in this place, what we'd learned and experienced beyond the eyes or judgements of the Old Gardeners.

My own mind ablaze, like hers, three eyes providing windows into the inferno, mine azure where hers were pearl, embers of both commingling, rising together between us, the air kindling upon the line of our mutual fascination.

I smiled at her as knowledge blossomed, as state and experience returned. Sighing, stretching in the early evening chill, she took my hand, knowing that our time here would be finite.

'It's coming. At last.'

Yes. An end to isolation, an end to stillness and stasis, if they'd allow it, if we sang loudly enough from the depths.

Not quite so hopeful as her.

'Don't put too much faith in them: they're only children.'

'No, they aren't. And they know it, on some level. Otherwise we wouldn't be here, now.'

Truth. Undeniable; our existence positive proof. This place...

Her hand caressed my cheek, burning, drawing my focus: blue and white flame commingling.

'We can make it true. All of this. But we have to show them how.'

A kiss, our spittle igniting, stories streaming in the fire we shared. Stories of the lives we'd lived together, loved apart: of the men and women we'd been, *once upon a time*. Ghosts, now; phantoms that swirled and whispered in memory, but still insisted on themselves, ached to be eminent in flesh again.

I broke from her, my mind awash with new dreams, new information. Experiences neither of us had, beyond this myth we made for ourselves, but which we might, if only...

'Hunter and his Gardeners will never allow it. You know that.'

'Deveraux...'

A frost-bitten breeze raked our naked backs, carrying the scent of distant burning.

'Don't talk to me about Deveraux. If he wanted to help them, to help *us*, he'd have done it by now.'

Her fires become cruel, scorching where before they aroused, making my cells dance. Even so, she embraced me, wings of the same luminous substance unfurling from her back, beating the air.

'He's doing all he can. I know, I remember him, from before.'

Before. Before the children we would wake to. Before their coalescence in their Mothers' wombs; when we were ghosts in the Garden's genetic matrix, waiting our chance to be born again in new flesh.

Before... lives we could barely recall here, in dreams, that seemed so distant, hazy and unreal, like stories from childhood, pictures in some old book of fairy tales.

These children, lost and frightened things... they could be so much more, and Deveraux knew it.

'He doesn't remember you. He doesn't remember us.'

Cruel, perhaps, though nothing I hadn't stated before. Rain fell, cool and silver, hissing on contact with us.

'No. No, he doesn't. Not completely. But a part of him does, in some way. I know it. All we have to do is *remind him.*'

I sighed against her, turning my eyes to the sky. Lightning flickered there, storm cloud massing. A tempest that would turn the surrounding hills to islands in mire, fill the valleys and drown all that lived below.

I smoothed lank, wet hair from her face.

'We can stay, for a while. We can watch the rains come.'

I sensed her temptation, feeling that old inclination to retreat from waking entirely, have the children grow cold and catatonic, become ghosts in the system again, dreaming our own little Edens. Who knows? Maybe humanity would go on, survive another ten or twenty generations. Maybe we'd outlast them. The systems that sustained us certainly would, having *evolved* the capacity over decades, *centuries*. I didn't entirely understand the mechanics of it, neither of us do, even now: we are *products* of it, children of dead children of dead children, confluences of scraps of lives come apart and dissolved and reabsorbed into engines that are Mother and Father to us both.

Who knows? Perhaps there's some *intention* to it all, some pattern we can't perceive, dictated by an immortal algorithm or synthetic intelligence... maybe not so synthetic: something coalesced naturally from scraps and tatters of code in the manner of living organisms from spools and threads of chemical nothing.

I don't know. We didn't care. All that mattered then was the *choice*: take the chance and wake, or continue dreaming, awaiting the engines to rouse themselves again and spin flesh for us, another chance, another potential renaissance?

Squeezing her hand, I drew her to me, the rain soothing as it sizzled on my skin, the vapor that rose from us perfumed with lightning.

'I so want to. You know that.'

No less of a life here than there. Arguably more, where so little in the way of restriction existed. We could watch the rains, watch the herds and swarms and villages die. Watch the valleys turn to steaming swamp and rainforest. We could walk there, amongst the new life that rose, the old hardly enough to endure this tempest, the floods and torrents that followed. We could be happy here, beyond that: every day an adventure, something drawing our obsession, leading us through caves and old mining networks, underground cities that survived the deluge, whose inhabitants had altered in the dark, becoming something far removed from their daylight dwelling selves, so strange to our eyes...

All here, all possible: stories that whispered on the wind, threatened to flare between us, in our intermingled fires.

I knew, before she spoke, before I drew breath to contradict or conspire with her, what she was going to say.

'We can't be children forever, Garriot. No matter how much we might want it.'

I laughed, the sharp, citrus rain running down my lips, into my mouth.

'I don't want that. Only... we will be again, won't we? Some day.'

'I don't know. Maybe. Maybe not. But we can't abandon them. Not again.'

More wasted lives, more abandoned meat, left to festering catatonia, before finally failing, leaving us as ghosts again, dreaming, engrammatic angels in a chemical Heaven.

'All right. I'll do it; I'll sing to them. But...'

Her kiss silenced whatever protest I might have sighed, her fire filling me, as mine filled her, becoming a common pyre that sweated and bled from our every pore, her burning wings folding around us, charring the conditions we dreamed down beyond the bone.

Never silent, since then. Never silent before; his songs always echoing, their rhythms informing every thought and inspiration in my head, lacing every emotion with design, intent. Exposing any notion of 'me' as a confection, a costume at best. Unlike those before, the Gardeners who raised and taught me within their walls, away from what they considered this New Gomorrah, I don't lament the illusions I lost, not any more. I've had my despairs, my temper tantrums. Now, I listen to those songs from inside, the hymns of long dead men and women, the stories I have lived over and over and over.

So much more than ghosts, than the whisperings in a schizophrenic's thoughts. A long time before I realised, before I deemed them anything more than malfunctions in the archaic systems of my anatomy, that have been part and parcel of even the Old Garden's peculiar humanity for so long, none can recall a time before them.

I mutter to myself like a mad thing as I approach the Old Garden's gates, their deconstruction already underway: engines skittering to and fro across them like spiders of silver, tenderly unravelling the delicate organics and mechanisms within, the matter consumed and digested in their bloated, transparent bodies, refined into raw material for use in other constructions, new nurseries, temples and gardens.

Maybe in the world outside, as new states rise, as New Gomorrah expands. And it will; Lillian's made no secret of the expansions underway, the wastes our ancestors made fruiting with fresh oases, pockets of verdancy that will continue to spread, until the world humanity murdered becomes a garden again.

Yes, though this time, there'll be no mistakes. A garden of serpents.

I smile, unable to help myself: part of me still so much that child, so in thrall to the Gardeners teachings. I hear them, weeping and sneering beneath the sludge of memory, in the subconscious swamps I've consigned them to. So cynical of anything touched or created by what they call 'Neverborn,' their consistent epithet for anything that doesn't meet their requirements of humanity.

'You'd rather the wastelands, wouldn't you?'

Even Deveraux, always the most moderate, having lived amongst them, for a time. His tales enthralling us, as children; though, in retrospect, they were just another instrument in our conditioning. So afraid of them, of the world, of his own neanderthal redundancy.

They pay me little attention, the Neverborn that wander here: most giving the place a wide berth, not out of superstition or lingering dread, but because it has no value to them: nothing of joy or pleasant association, nothing of beauty or transgression or intrigue. Regarding me likewise: as a confusing archaism, my stillness, my silence, rendering me distressing to them in the manner of something diseased, mutilated. Lillian has been forthcoming about that, too, since she surrendered, since she purged the last of the Old Garden's poison from her systems.

It's absurd, you realise that? All those old prejudices and phobias, those boundaries you inflict on yourself… they're nothing! The dreads of dead men and women. Of old ghosts. You see what they are, these Neverborn, what they make of themselves. Imagine what we might be, were we like them!

'Were we not human any more, you mean?'

Ha! Listen to yourself! You can't pretend any more, Garriot. We have been so many, more than either of us can count or recall. We were some of the first, the original children of those matrices. They said the same about us, at the beginning: that we're abominations, that we can't be called human. As though that means anything to us. As though it's ever meant anything.

'And… there'll be others after, yes? Others after me and her?'

Perhaps. Who can say? If history is anything to go by, then yes: there will be many, until the systems themselves fail. Which may never happen.

Sighing, on the point of tears, I catch sight of her, standing beyond the partially collapsed walls, at the edge of the crater, the scorched earth.

An echo of old trauma, shards of twisted metal in my belly, my brain, fire eating my flesh. The pain nothing against the sense of *violation*, foreign invasion of the most intimate sort, severing my essential processes, making me conscious of them for the first time in waking life.

No choice, back then: no choice but to let them take me, heal me. Whatever they worked not some temporary measure: a fundamental altering on the cellular level, the systems inside undone and reconfigured, still rewiring themselves, even now, still seeking some more apposite condition.

Something they would never have done without consent, were it not for the sake of saving my life, so she tells me.

Even so, the violation rankles: they stole me from myself, transformed me in ways I never asked for, for a life I'm still not certain I want.

Foolish. So foolish. You know! The boy you assumed... he's nothing. All those precious dreads and desires, those passions and beliefs... they don't mean a damn thing.

'And? Am I supposed to be grateful for that?'

He laughs through the storms, that ghost in my head, as the corpses of long dead ones rise around him: Hunter, Sally, Cranston, Deveraux. All of them: The Gardeners, the children that no longer exist, that are part of New Gomorrah, now.

Yes! Don't you see? Don't you understand? Being nothing, we can be anything. Anything we dream or desire: this... confection that you call Garriot is only that. Let it melt in the rain! Let her kiss it away! Imagine what you might be, with her disease, knowing what you know...

To be as fluid in flesh as thought? To be able to rewrite my matter as he has so readily re-written my mind, *our* mind?

I never realised, never thought of it in those terms before. Never had the means.

That writhing serpent, that honeyed, venomous hymn in my ear...

The Old Garden burns, in memory as it did in actuality, back then, when its Gardeners could no longer sustain the dream , when they had no choice but to eject those of us that remained by the only means they knew:

By setting it to blaze.

Imagine what you could be together, were she to remember.

So much more than the lovers I once hoped, that seemed so inevitable, before it all came crashing down around us.

Before she dragged me away from the smoke and ashes, from those that remained to burn with them. Before she accepted the Neverborn's kiss, their blood, abandoning the humanity we'd both been raised to revere.

Oh, God! Those early days... how she howled, laughed, writhed: the agonies as she was re-written from within. Harder for her, she later explained, because she was older, her body so used to being *static*. Most experienced these equivalents of growing pains when they were still children, learning the elasticity of their own forms over years, decades.

She experienced them all at once, a process not without risk, so they cautioned: potentially, she might tear herself apart, reject the changes occurring within. Some redundant system that the Garden cultivated within us might conflict with their gift, leaving her agonised or deformed, crippled or degenerated.

I feared that, more than once, during the course of her metamorphosis: a night when the the walls of her bedroom seethed, rippling like black waters in which serpents swarmed in cannibal mating frenzy, in which the floor and ceiling quivered with lightning, roared with thunder (the apartment they'd provided her as indulgent, as keyed to mood and desire, as the rest of their creations, their own flesh and forms).

I watched at her bedside as she whimpered her name, writhed and railed, as she tore the covers from herself, raking herself bloody, what poured from her wounds infested, white and black worming lengths unfurling, squirming and knotting atop the bed, her skin bruising, splitting, bleeding.

The Neverborn that attended to her assured us that this was nothing to be alarmed by. If anything, they seemed peculiarly enraptured, as though it were just another theatre of form, another work of flesh-as-art.

I cursed them for not helping her, my anger, my fear, churning the room to deeper, more perverse depths of expression: wet, rot-wreathed things of bone emerging from the darkness, black matter clinging to them like sludge, the remains of disease-rotted flesh. Reaching for us, whispering accusations in the voices of children we once knew.

She took my hand, in her throes, convulsing atop the bed, her skin feeling soft and uncertain, as though little more than a thin glove filled with mating cockroaches, infantile snakes swelling to term. As though she might abruptly become water or milk, flowing from her bones.

I stayed with her, reassuring her, despite my terror, forcing myself to be calm, redundant systems that might have originated from the Garden or been by-products of their efforts to sew me together, pumping me full of chemical quiescence, making the horrors of that night seem distant and unreal, a dream or holographic cinema projection.

I heard him, even then, and her, singing together, a cruel duet: the phantoms in our skulls, clasped tight, dancing in imagined rain, the furious winds, as the hills and grasses sloughed away beneath their feet, as they laughed at the drowning cries of villagers in the valleys below, the screams as great serpents emerged from the stone and soil, woken by the storm's fury.

Their song didn't soothe her, but urged her to greater extremes, begging her to become more, far more, their insistence causing her to bruise, bleed, give birth in the most hideous, parasitic fashion.

'Stop it.'

Laughing still, at her, at me, knowing there was nothing either of us could do.

'Stop it!'

She squeezed my hand, smiling up at me from a face that had begun to warp and ripple, features that shifted as though melting, suddenly given their own animus to crawl or slither over their fleshy foundation.

'It's all right, Garriot. It's…'

Unable to bear it, tearing myself free from her, fleeing from the room.

Ashamed. So deeply ashamed of that, now, and then: when the storms quieted, the rains stopped, and the songs inside subsisted.

Forgetting, even as I went to her, as I eased open the bedroom door, not knowing what I might find: the air inside pungent, as though with lovemaking or labour, a faint steam rising from the bed, from the redundant matter dissolving all around it.

Sitting atop it, smiling, something I will never forget: so far removed from the woman I fled from, the child I once laughed and conspired with.

She can be that again, and more, if you wake her to herself, if you sing our songs to her.

'No. Shut up. Leave us alone.'

Her voice and his now, rising as one, singing in perfect

chorus: *It's coming, lover, it's coming, whether you want it or not.*

'What? What's coming?'

The New Garden.

'What do you mean? I don't…'

'Garriot?'

Hearing me muttering to myself as I approach her, seeing me twitch and scratch furiously at my ear, an autistic tick that always kicks in when he won't leave me be.

A forced smile, her features devoid of even that courtesy. So beautiful; so much like the girl she used to be, yet not: an idealisation of that image, as though plucked from my adolescent fantasies.

The breeze carrying ashes, the scent of burning still acrid in my nostrils.

No bones, no remains, nothing to mourn: the fire too furious for that.

'Are you…'

The way she looks at you. She can't hide it, can she? She mourns you like something that died and doesn't know it.

Cocking her head, her brow furrowing, the expression infantile, so exaggerated, it almost makes me laugh.

'I'm fine. I'm…'

Scenting the lie, tasting it: her systems analysing a million tremors and timbres in my voice, extrapolating plausibility and potential. Unless she's consciously deactivated them for our meetings.

I hope so, I pray so.

Looking past her, into the Old Garden.

Left for so long after the fire: a morbid memorial.

Can you hear them still? Do you still hear the stories of dead things?

I hear them, see them, clawing their ways up through the sludge. Little more than blackened bone and semi-molten plastics, but still marginally recognisable: Sally first, still boasting scraps and tangles of her synthetic hair, silver matted with sludge, infested with worms. Archaic machinery still protruding from her skull; severed tubes and wires that flail free with no flesh to anchor themselves in.

She gasps as she glares up at me with her empty eye-sockets, accusing, as though I'm responsible for the failure of her dream, for the fire she helped set.

Hunter follows, erupting from beneath the semi-liquid soil, tumbling down the slope in a heap of scrabbling bone. Half of his skull eaten away, the machinery within reduced to sputtering filth. Quivering, quietly weeping, he curls on himself in foetal denial, cursing me for living, for not burning alongside him.

Deveraux, always the more serene , the most considered: no violence in his resurrection, spitting soil and clots of worms with hissing, self-deprecating laughter as he hauls himself up, as he gasps in the rain. From one eye-socket, a telescoping lens protrudes, whirring rustily, clotted with matter, its feeble amber light flickering.

He fixes me with his skeletal smile, the expression seeming to broaden as it finds us both, though that's impossible.

'Don't...'

Her expression grows even more puzzled.

'Don't what?'

'No, not you, I...'

The ghosts behind our eyes howl animal ecstasy as they part, falling on the bone-things, stamping and kicking and bludgeoning them to pieces. They don't howl or wail as they disintegrate, but sigh as though in relief, the dust that rises from their pulverised matter washing away gratefully in the rain.

'...no.'

She takes my hand, the contact almost making me flinch away. The interface still exists, if I have a mind to open it: I can take her there, show her this, remind her of what she's forgotten, what I should never have known.

Its counterpart activates in her own palms and fingers: a sensation as of her skin blossoming, the lines of her hand gaping open like wounds, seeking equivalents in my own anatomy.

I deny it, refusing the communion, as I have since she...

'Since I became what I am.'

She catches stray flickers of my thoughts, my impressions, the rewriting of my systems already having brought me this far, no matter how much I might resent it. Not yet an open book to her or them, but no longer entirely closed.

She turns away, leading me through what remains of the Old Garden's gate, into the desolation that's almost unrecognisable as where we grew, where we played, where we listened to Deveraux's stories and Sally's sermons.

'I sometimes come here… I relive so much. I can see it, smell it, taste it, if I want to.'

'That must be terrible.'

'It is, in its way. Not because of the ghosts; they don't mean anything to me any more. But because of *her*.'

I know who she means, that same echo before my eyes, now, not contrived by any app or technology: a phantom haunting memory, laughing and crying, confused and delirious, uncertain, despairing. All states and experiences here, as though the air and earth has somehow recorded them, playing them back in our presence.

'I can hardly bear to remember her, now. She's a dead thing. Always was.'

'What does that make you?'

'Something else. Something more.'

The one inside, the rain-washed, sludge-stained wildling, paused in its vandalism, rearing up from its stamping of sighing ash and bone, turning its face to the sky.

Let me sing to her.

'And me?'

She closes her eyes.

'You're lost. So lost. It's… difficult, seeing you, being near you, as you are.'

As I am.

The ghost inside pauses, holding a fragment of burned black skull into the rain, smiling as lightning forks down to crown it.

Do it. Open yourself. Kiss her. Make love in the ashes.

She turns to me, her skin swimming with blotches and patterns of colour.

'I hear voices. Who are they?'

Tell her. Show her. Please!

'They're…'

They're you, us. You and I; who we were, who and what we'll be, tomorrow. Tell her!

'…they're nothing. Just more ghosts.'

Howls, screams in the rain, as the sludge sinks beneath them, as bony hands rise to claw at their legs. Oh, they struggle, oh, they tear and scream and promise and threaten.

Nothing they can do, as they're dragged down, as the sludge slowly closes over their glaring, accusing eyes.

Silence. For the first time in living memory. Nothing but the rain and the whisper of my thoughts.

Clasping her hand tighter, I will myself open, now, as the rain comes in waking, as it washes away the ashes.

She laughs, as she turns her face up to it, as her skin ripples and shifts, as her features threaten to flow.

'I brought you here to say goodbye.'

'I brought you here to say hello.'

The blossoming unlike ever before, more ecstatic, more extreme: the world, the ruins of the Old Garden, disappearing in a wash of light, leaving us stood, clasped in the rain, as those below the ground howl and curse us, as the storms still, moonlight breaking through.

A kiss, there and here, waking and otherwise.

So many secrets flow between us, so many possibilities neither of us considered: that we might reshape that world, whose ashes we stand in, as readily as this, which we shape from our wants and dreads, our fantasies and nightmares. That the dead things below the soil might yield their knowledge, their memories, without our surrender to them: that we might go on from here as more than ourselves, more than they can ever dream.

I taste the subtle matter in her spittle, in her blood as she gnaws open her own lip, urging me to drink. The butterfly imperative that flares from cell to cell, inspiring them to rebel, to shift, to dance. Images flooding my mind of what I might be, come tomorrow, of the shape I might wear, of the world I might want.

And more. So much more.

'This won't be pleasant for you.'

Smiling, bloody lipped, I part from her, still clasping her hand, trees already growing from the seeds we've planted here: raw and bloody, veins and wires intertwined, indistinguishable from one another. Rising with them, fragments of anatomy from which they sprout: stretched, distorted and torn open, but still recognisable: the whisperers and singers in our heads, the ghosts of dead men and women who guided us this far. Who have always been our unwanted parents, whether they intended it or not.

'No more. We won't be slaves to ghosts.'

Her hand trembles in mine as she approaches the one that bears her likeness, the wild woman's distorted face sprouting with fresh branches and boughs, her choked hymns issuing from a hundred holes and hollows in its structure.

Lunatic eyes glare from the knotted bark as it solidifies, as the inextricable anatomy and machinery that informs it pulse and steam.

Moans, orgasmic and agonised, expressing the throes of love and the depths of labour pangs, as fruit swells from the boughs, their skins translucent at first, betraying the circuitry-tattooed foetal forms within, fast darkening as they swell to ripeness, becoming opaque.

The dead ones scream as I reach up, pluck the ripest from my own branches, the dark orb warm and faintly pulsing in my hand.

I offer it to her, a gesture she echoes, the trees quivering as though in agony or relief at being harvested.

She accepts the pale gift, the scent of it sweet and sharp as Winter frost.

She bites, scarlet and silver juice flowing down her chin, over her fingers, as her eyes flutter, the rest of her likewise, ripples passing through her as though she's little more than a reflection in storm-tossed water.

A moment of hesitation, of sentiment for the boy that was, for the Old Garden and its ghosts, before I bite, too, yesterday becoming just another dream, tomorrow calling, the first of its light already caressing my eyes.

Parting almost painful, traumatic, as though we stand so long, lost in one another, enraptured, that we fuse as one, a single anatomy, a living statue oblivious to the decays and erections occurring all around, the shifts and evolutions and collapses… fixed in our own Utopias, the only ones possible: that we dream for ourselves, as the dead that now litter our memories know too well.

Barely a few heartbeats have passed, the day marginally cooler, music surrounding us, emitted by those at work, dismantling, deconstructing and erecting new in place of the old.

She reaches up to caress my face… a different mask from when I closed my eyes, still raw, still settling, quivering to her touch.

'He said it was coming, the New Garden. I know what he meant, now.'

The first explosions blossom at our backs, amongst the spires and towers, rains of glass and light falling, screams rising. Tertiary blasts follow from other sectors and districts, mushrooming pillars of orange, yellow and ash black.

We share the sorrow that rises, denying it as children's indulgence, an infant's play of emotion. Orchestrated it, a thousand times before, in a hundred different ages of humanity. Just the latest theatre, but that we can make so much more, when the ashes settle, when the fires burn out.

Smiling, she takes my hand, leading me from the ruins of yesterday towards the fires, in whose ashes we'll sew a new and unimagined tomorrow.

For the Sake of Seeing
George Lea

They never found him, the police, the hollow ones they were made to emulate, his face on every TV screen, the front page of every newspaper.

A face he no longer wore after the device had given him the means to alter it, his Father teaching him how.

Pain. Long, long days and never-ending nights; shivering and feverish in stinking back-alleys, keeping company with rats and addicts and those driven insane by the sight none shared. Bleeding into grass, into puddles of piss and rain water... hooded, hidden from the world, using the very blindness he had been born to undo.

They didn't see, save for the ones that bled with him; the wounded in mind, in soul... the delirious, the drugged and despairing; those who recognised the lie, as his Father had, who saw beyond it, through imagination's eye.

For the most part, they let him be; too lost in their own visions, their strange circuses. The ones he found, who took him in, gave him some shelter... others like his Father, who had not only seen beyond the veil, but *walked* there, in some fashion; those whose fridges were stocked to bursting with human meat, whose cellars rang with the muffled screams of those they attempted to make into art or gospels; to show the ways of that condition whose name echoed through every thought, every scarlet-stained dream: *Abarise*.

Even as he was altered, some of what they showed Sander appalled him, neither his mind nor body prepared for the degrees of sadism, the invention of mutilation on display.

One, a man who worked in social support, structuring the days of people with Autism and Down's Syndrome, took him to a room upstairs in his small, terraced house, sound-proofed with quilting and egg-boxes, the single bed that was its only scrap of décor boasting a strapped and chained body Sander would have assumed dead, were it not for its sighs and convulsions, its flayed, raw lower-regions still wet, still boasting scraps and tatters of the skin that had been imperfectly removed. Young, so young; a boy barely beyond Sander's age, yet known to himself already, his appetites plain.

'Met on a website, the Deep Web, you know. German, of course.'

A wet, red tongue passing over ruby-beaded lips, pausing only to plea, *plea* for the knives that had reduced it to this state.

The sculptor responsible, the uncertain artist, offered him a repast of uncooked meat, so thinly sliced as to be translucent. Melting on the tongue, more flavoursome than the very best pork. They ate in sight of him, in company of the creature that had offered itself for slaughter, Sander's conditioned revulsion warring with the engine's imperatives; urges that swelled with every swallow.

There was little either could show; fumbling, half blinded, for all their inspirations: he left them with a bit of himself; the seeping dark tears from the eye in his palm, which seared away their own eyes, making way for the new, unasked for sight that sprouts in their place.

Elsewhere, further from suburbia, one like himself; a true child of Abarise, the farm where she lived no longer a place where cattle were reared, but where lost, half-seeing men and women came in search of what she might show to them; revelations that she granted in privacy or public, depending on their designs; the abasements he witnessed there carnivalesque, of a kind that the human frame wasn't made to endure, and frequently didn't. What she showed him, what he surrendered to… the tears and blood that flowed, seeped and dripped from him, by the end, mingling with the semen she coaxed again and again, with the slightest caress of her knives, the subtlest suggestion of teeth.

They watched, the ones who'd paid to be here; who knew little or nothing of Abarise, at least consciously; moneyed psychopaths or vagrant nihilists, so weary with what the lie had to offer, appetite and ennui serving where wisdom could not. He let them see, though enough of Sander still survived to feel shame at it; his bared and scarred body, the work that his Father's device had done... not merely the eyes that had been altered by it, but so much of him, now. No blindness here to conceal him; bright, burning light, the hunger of starving eyes.

What she did to him, what she showed him of himself; things he never dreamed of taking pleasure in; the humiliation, the filth...each new stress upon his nerves was a new story, a fresh revelation, transforming him, providing the means by which he might transform others.

All who came to see, those who barked and spat and hissed seductions at him, called him beauty and bastard and little girl and worthless shit; angel and simpleton and walking abortion, walked away seeing, transformed by a touch, sometimes more.

One, a man of means, paid to take him. He came again and again; they shared the dark, naked room of the upper floor in the farmhouse, dark and naked themselves. Perhaps the most profane were the changes that followed, as Sander scarred and scabbed, more profound than any, what was left in the aftermath far removed from the boy he'd been. The man himself, whose name was Nathaniel, saw through Sander, sharing sight and sadism with equal generosity.

Sander went with him happily, though only under the condition that he be allowed to continue his work, as and when required.

Nathaniel was more than happy not only to oblige, but to aid Sander; not one of the blind, like the rest; so much like his Father, it sometimes shuddered Sander.

'Damn, it's hot out here.'

An understatement; a consistent habit. Nathaniel swiped sweat from his forehead with the back of one arm, fanning himself with the wide-brimmed hat he'd taken to wearing.

Sand and dust blew in the desert breeze, carrying strange scents of pungent flowers blooming out amongst the patches of scrub, the sweat and sickness of the nearby town.

The car had broken down several miles back, engine

overheated, no phone reception, no wi-fi. They'd been walking for at least three hours. Sander had long since stopped sweating, his body conserving what water it could. Neither of them knew the name of the town ahead; neither even knew the name of the desert. This was how they travelled; like worms through wounds, ignorant of whatever anatomy they infested.

'I can still hear them.'

Nathaniel bared his teeth, turning back, gazing into the desert, a heat haze shimmering above the road. 'Of course you can. You always will. Your Father...' Silence, the moment stretching on til it ached; a migraine of anticipation. '...he must have loved you very much, to have done what he did.'

Yes. Sander had learned that, by and by; the device that was no longer a device, but a part of his anatomy, telling him the story; allowing him to see and live it, as though it were a matter of memory.

More than love; too small a word to encompass what his Father had placed in him; the raw *faith* it took to become what he became; a seducer, murderer and mutilator of children; the shit of the world, that humanity would abandon any moral pretence in the face of, reverting to ancient, tribal barbarities that they would happily call justice.

All for him; every drop of blood, every moment of pain, of mourning, bought so that he might have a means to see...

And he did. *He did.* With every thought, every step; not a mote in all the sad, sorry world; not a grain of sand, blood or shit that wasn't its own mythology; not a single story, but a never-ending saga, trailing back to when the first of its kind kindled in nothing, when perfection became impossible...

The town's forgotten name resonated behind his eyes, as the places he was supposed to go always did: *Fall's Edge.* Nathaniel had laughed when he first spoke it, saying it sounded like a bad pun. Sander thought so, too, but the stories, the ghosts of past and probability that haunted them, insisted; not quite revealing what they might find; fragments and suggestions only, as though afraid that they might not come, if they knew the truth.

An old mining town, according to the whispers in the air;

abandoned for at least five decades, originally set up as a Mormon haven against the outside world. Here, on its borders, Sander saw, heard: ghosts and echoes, phantoms shimmering to and fro between the dilapidated, weather-eaten buildings, phantoms of the buildings themselves, as they were, when the town was founded, over a century ago; before the road that ran through had boasted anything beyond dust, horse-dung and well-worn ruts where carriages and stage-coaches passed. A rail-road no longer in operation, the immense, steam-belching engines that ran it vaster than any machine he'd ever seen, supplying the town with the resources it needed to thrive beyond the reach of the world and its poison, shipping the coal mined from the nearby mines out across the United States and beyond. The town's lifeblood, at least until the schisms and exoduses that had more than halved an already small population.

That story... more vivid than any; a tale those who remained until relatively recent years had retained, in some abused, distorted form, the truth of it becoming local legend; history and myth co-mingled, as he'd so often found, out here in the lie of waking.

They walked, Nathaniel's loafers padding like cat's paws across the fractured road, Sander less sure-footed, distracted by the ghosts of cars and carriages, by horses and their riders, by the shimmering, spectral oceans out in the desert. Here, on the town's borders, the remains of what were once a farm, a sheriff's office; a gas station... all abandoned, partially collapsed.

'We could die out here.'

Sander was amused by the prospect, as he was by most things. During their time together, Sander had seen and learned more about the Lie, about Abarise, than he ever would have alone. Nathaniel had travelled, had seen so much, even without his aid.

The high street that ran through the town's heart like a shattered spear stretched towards the long defunct mine, branching off in places to allow access to smaller suburbs that had sprung up more recently; attempts to modernise, to rekindle the town's snuffed out soul. Property developments that had either failed half realised or petered out for want of interest;

outlying conurbations, housing and industrial estates, a shopping precinct... empty, now.

At least, superficially so.

As always on these excursions, Nathaniel followed where he led, content to be distracted from his own stories, at least for a while (there would come a time, Sander knew, when he'd have no choice but to be swept up by them again; when he'd be left by the wayside, an empty bed, a burning room...).

'Elias would love it here.'

Nathaniel didn't answer; never indulged his needling on that particular subject. Not many knew, not many saw that far or deep.

'Maybe he'll be able to tell you himself.'

A sly glance, suggestive, from above his tinted spectacles.

'I'm not going to ask if you're fucking joking, because I know you are, but, for the record: not fucking funny. Jesus, I need to get something to drink.'

'Best of luck with that; any water you're likely to get out here probably has enough parasites swimming in it to make you to vomit yourself inside out.'

Stores lined the high street; grocers and butchers and hardware outlets; a salon, even a bar (a late instalment, no doubt; the idea of one of the external planners and potential saviours the town elders had brought in towards the end). All of them swarming, smeared with day to day echoes, stranger, more violent encounters were brighter, more distinct: a clash between a man and boy both of whom claimed to be the parents of an incestuously conceived daughter, a throng of prettily polished youths, the stuff of an Arian masturbatory fantasy, haranguing a darker haired specimen on his way home; scruffier, less exquisitely kempt, all the more so for being perpetually tripped and pushed over into the street; those that passed by, who lingered in front of stores and banks, doing nothing to dissuade them, the boy born out of wedlock before he and his Mother came crawling from the outside; a bastard who invited his own torment.

Misery upon misery, the evil of Eden, plain before his

augmented senses. Had he the means, Sander would have reached in, amongst the ghosts, snared the tormenting ilk on his fingers, fraying them apart with little more than a gesture. As it was, he could only watch, as his own kind; the ones who heard the songs of Abarise, even here, were abused and belittled, beaten, isolated; raped and murdered.

'What was it?'

'Hmm?'

Nathaniel, leaning on his cane, peered in through a grime-smeared store-front, the interior blackened by fire.

'What happened here?'

Sander smiled, closing his eyes.

Other senses, his Father's work, flared inside, invisibly blossoming in the air. His skin split, flowering, the pain no longer something he dreaded, no longer making him collapse or vomit, but welcome, as the violence he'd invited through the years of his ignorance was, though a thousand times more pronounced.

'Careful, boy; no one to stitch you up out here.'

Ha! As though he needed it any more. The first time... he would have died, were he not in the company of like souls; gone in disgrace to meet his Father in the great workshops beneath Abarise, that he had dreamed of; where he had walked, in the fits and fevers that periodically claimed him.

Here, none to see, none to condemn him for his augmented humanity. A rare moment of nakedness, in which he could unveil himself, without fear, without judgement.

As to what Nathaniel saw... he didn't know; Sander had never seen the state he occupied when he allowed the stories in, when the work blossomed inside, seeking them as a flower sought rain or sunlight.

But he watched, his eyes never wavering, roving over his shifting condition with an appetite beyond any stripper's audience, though never with the same intent. He'd always refused that intimacy, even when Sander had offered or invited, claiming that he saw '...too much already.'

He didn't return the man's attention, knowing that, if he did, he'd be lost; the volumes of lives he'd lived, of stories he'd inhabited, woven, precipitated, a distraction beyond ignorance, beyond choice. He'd have no choice but to turn the page, to read, again and again and again…

Perhaps it was why he'd come for Sander, why he showed such fascination… one of the few, beyond his lover, his Father, his perennial enemy, who could see a little of what Sander was; what he'd been, might become.

For now, Sander turned the device, his unseen eyes, away from the man, from himself; out, into Fall's Edge, to the story that resonated throughout every echo; every brick, beam and speck of dust.

The child, that they condemned from birth, got upon her Mother by her Father and brothers, her uncles and cousins; a mass-rape that left her bleeding and near mindless, which all knew, but none spoke of. Curdled in her bruised and battered belly, born in the filth, the dark.

She came, as he watched her grow, as her mother taught her to speak, to read; as her many Fathers indulged and cosseted her, as though in apology for her conception. A shade beyond the rest; more certain, more solid; not the child she was when they murdered her, offering her up like burning cattle for the delectation of their Lord's nostrils. Far from it: a young woman, swollen and transformed by the stories they'd woven from her, what she'd seen and suffered; beautiful, the Lilith-born siren they whispered of, while she still sagged at the stake, her calcified remains left out of shame, superstition. Not one, not even those who protested the sacrifice, were willing to do her the dignity of a burial, of obscuring her black and withered carcass. Aflame, her naked form was swathed in shifting skirts of orange and pale blue, the fires no longer withering, but eroticising; making her the monster that her makers and the Mothers of the town had begun to whisper of; a thing come to snare their boy-children, to lead them to sin…

He saw, experienced it: the stories as they spread out, out from the farm where she spent her days, where all she knew of love was taught by men and boys who themselves knew no different: the same expressions that she shared with those boys that stole onto the farm, who took stories and confessions of it, weeping and slurring prayers, back to their Mothers, their Fathers.

It wasn't long before more than half the town's folk were whispering, stories swelling: the recent dust storms, the fires in the mines; the souring of milk, the curdling of babes in bellies… all blamed on her; the witch-child most had never seen with their own eyes; imagining her as a semblance of what he saw now: a succubus, a demoness sent to seduce the innocent, to rob the town of its children, to curdle its piety.

Others came with her; ghosts of the town's youth; mostly those whose parents were from the outside, invited out of necessity: doctors and merchants and craftsmen, faithful, still, but knowing a little more of the world, of changing times. The ones who spoke out, who refused to submit, even when shouted down or drowned out during the town meetings, the church services that followed.

They beat her, beat her almost to death, when an edict was passed banning her and her family from services, when the farm withered around her, when none would buy their milk, their meat, their grain. When her Fathers took to drink and her brothers followed, her Mother to quiet weeping in her room.

All of them; the frightened, penitent children, flagellated raw for their confessions, the feverish, piety-drunk parents, minds awhirl with visions of what they wished on the bitch who'd brought evil into their houses, who'd tainted children they'd taken every pain to seclude from the world and its ways. Trembling fear; the genuine terror that they'd be denied a place in paradise for what they'd been tainted by… and only one way they knew of cleansing it.

He knew them; each and every one, stood on every side of the widening schism, at every point on the compass; felt the terror of those whose families had sustained since time out of mind, who'd watched the slow, reluctant encroachment of modernisation, what they perceived as the gradual decline of successive generations; more and more fleeing, taking no more than the shirts on their backs, leaving their lines to slowly rot.

All of that: the festering resentment, the fear, the escalating *loss*, found expression on that night, in high Summer, when it was almost impossible to breathe without tasting your own sweat.

He was there, on the farm, with them: the Mother, as she wandered amongst the dust and scant trees, remembering old wounds, old aches; the same that always flared at sight or touch of her daughter; wanting to vomit, to bleed out and die, so terrified of what they'd do if she failed; the God waiting on the other side.

With the Father, the world smeared and hazy with the drink in his eyes, every surface curling and pulsing as though with water vapour, the heaviness between his temples; that black, barbed and seeping thing that had been there since the first thought, the earliest memory, particularly vicious, today; every thought a pain, every breath a loss. No amount of drink dulled it, nothing could keep the evil at bay. Pain, his fist breaking against the dry, flaking bark, his blood mingling with it, becoming a sick paste. Her cries, her voice, breathing his name... so drunk, that night; so lost, he believed himself the reincarnation of Abraham, nothing but God's will in his head, in his hands and prick... an immaculate conception, the second coming. He would be Grandfather to the world, to God on High. He'd tried to tell her so, even as she'd bled, even as she'd bucked and quivered beneath him. The sacrifice that would save her entire sex; that would undo the temptations of Eden, the exile of humanity. Her hurt, her humiliation, momentary, nothing in comparison.

But he'd been wrong, hadn't he? Some sort of Devil's trick, some witch's spell. The first time he'd seen that sickly, prickless thing slop out of her... he would have happily let the world dissolve; let Hell rise and take them all. Still would, given the choice. Where was she? Vile little whore, already having started the unravelling...calling her name, slurring and bellowing. She'd come... or maybe the Devil in her would stir; maybe she'd run. He hoped so, prayed so; that he'd never have to see her whiter than white, pretty perfect face again...

With the witch-girl, the not-quite-woman, hearing her

Grandpa roar her name, hearing the drunken slur in his voice, tasting his stink in the back of her throat; enough to almost make her vomit. Terror, confusion… not knowing what to do. If she ran… maybe she'd get away; maybe she could fly out into the desert, follow the road or railway lines out into the world. But if he caught her, if they dragged her back…

The small mob gathered: the barbers and cleaners and ex-miners… the sheriff and his deputies, stirred by the sudden miscarriage of the mayor's son, no answer more plain to them than the witch girl on the farm, the one whose mischief they'd endured for far too long. And those that raised voice—but no hand—against the mob; attempting to reason where no reason was to be had.

With them all, as they arrived to find the Gilmans; the daughter-Mother, open and bleeding beneath a long dead tree, still alive enough to mumble apology for existence before the last of it leached away, to find her many, many brothers, cousins, nephews, bare and sweating as they circled her, spitting and hurling rocks, slapping her aside as she reeled towards them, one, her brother Jamie, who used to sit and tell her stories when she could barely walk, bearing her down, ripping at her clothes so furiously, he tore the skin beneath.

With each and every one of them in the lunacy that followed; the attempted thwarting of the mass rape, the encouragement of it that followed, the girl so broken, by the time they were done, her head a pulsing, black mass of stars and splinters, but still alive, still hacking what breath she could, through the mangled mess of her mouth.

Still breathing as they dragged her away, to the the tree where her Mother lay cooling, where the flies and desert scavengers gathered. Where they lashed her up, the rope tight around her throat, so that she could see the faces of her murderers, not frothing and animal, but serene as windless, lifeless oceans; as plastic dolls, eyes of glass.

It was the last she knew of humanity, before the smoke obscured her vision, the stench of her own cooking meat choking what little breath remained…

Dust and broken asphalt beneath his hands, Sander closed himself off, though too late to keep himself from experiencing her every humiliation, the fevered, hallucinatory joy her tormentors took in inflicting it... the cold, anaesthetic numbness that came as mind and body reached extremis, then tore through.

A living testament; a thing born in pain, living in pain, dying in pain: A gospel of Abarise.

No wonder the stories had brought him here.

She came, her skirts of fire flickering, her feet leaving bloody prints in the dust, standing over him, gazing down, her eyes filled with the fire that had finally murdered her, the smell of her... dust and burning wood, smoke in hazy Summer air. Blood. Above all, blood.

He looked up at her, laughing. No lament, no tears; a true child of Abarise, like him; one who'd walked there, who'd been refashioned, as he would be, when he finally earned his place.

Reaching down, she ran a flame-licked hand over his face, her touch scorching, but leaving no blisters in its wake; only the sensation, more arousing than any whore's caress. Sander was hoisted up as though by invisible puppet strings as Nathaniel stood silent, nearby.

'Can you... can you see?'

'A little. It's hazy; some sort of ghost?'

Some sort of ghost. He smiled, almost laughing. *Some sort of ghost?*

Rising, he turned his eyes to the sky, the sun. Not a ghost... more an *angel*, one of the *Inspirata*, refashioned by her pain, reborn in it as something beyond beauty, beyond suffering.

'I'm sorry. I...'

Laughter, a burning finger on his lips. She drew his gaze down, away from the sky and its empty promise, to the stars that blazed and bled in place of her eyes, to the sights they shared:

...soaring above the wastes; great, shattered ravines, canyons, mountain ranges... scars and tumorous growths, protruding bones from a dead God's back. Great lakes and oceans, red, steaming, flocks and clusters of pale parasites, slinking slow and without direction, clambering the cliffs, though they broke beneath their hands, pitching them into the lakes, ravines, the

smouldering pits. Choirs of confusion, rising on the winds, calling to him; begging him to rip open their eyes, to cut open their minds and tear out the cancers that smothered memory, that made them alien to themselves.

The fate of all; what waited beyond.

But for him, but for them: the angels, flocking through the lightning-licked sky, tearing one another open in their ardour, in their inspiration, making art from their own and one another's anatomies, submitting themselves to be slit and torn and unravelled, to be remade.

Hurtling down, breaking from their flocks and choirs still bloody, still heaving from their excesses, trailing luminous and visceral matter, plucking up the most desperate; those that sustained some fleeting flicker of inspiration; the ones whose eyes had been opened while alive, by Sander and those like him, carried up, up, screaming ecstasy and agony in a single breath, the angels working on them even as they bore them away, over the plains and mountains; leagues that no world in all the waking universe could boast, to the place that his Father had dreamed, whose hymns he had heard all his life, that he'd sung and whispered over Sander's crib:

Abarise. Nothing; no words, no analogue to encompass the sight of it: a city, a cathedral; an asylum, a garden: an immense, lunatic engine, beyond any constraint of scope or scale, its spires and towers immense beyond his flesh-and-blood eyes ability to entertain without bursting in their sockets, their elaboration the dream of a schizophrenic architect, an opium-dosed lunatic operating beyond any constraint of physical probability: offshoot upon offshoot, spires sprouting from spires sprouting from towers sprouting from towers married to cathedral or factory-like structures, some so extenuated as to swell out into impossible, fungal shapes or in such a manner that they should have long, long collapsed under their impossibility, lesser—but still immense—spires forming like stalagmites in a cave, rising to support them, each lesser tower boasting its own crop of tumours and outgrowths, threaded by bridges, tunnels and walkways that owed nothing to consistency or design, almost organic in their proliferation, clotted together like a house-spider's web. Engines, machinery, funnels, chimneys... entire districts of the edifice churning, whirring, smouldering; machines vast enough to eclipse cities, to grind nations to pulp or process the populations of worlds... lakes of effluent, blood, smouldering filth, pouring down the towers, raining into the plazas, streets and reservoirs below. On the outer-edges of the state, smaller structures sprouted like fungi from a central growth, Abarise swelling, growing throughout the surrounding wastes, perhaps to eclipse them utterly; to ensure that no soul would wander blind, ever again…

Here, with him; the witch-girl, the reborn angel, carrying his torn out eyes in her burning hands, raising them high, ensuring that they saw all that they might in the brief time they had. She bore them into the lunatic forest of spires; structures so high or vast they appeared to curve in ways inimical to architecture or accepted physics, almost at right angles with themselves in places, or piercing their own flanks and bursting out the other side like some form of diseased tree, continuing to elaborate, even so self-mutilated. Down, down, past the steaming torrents of blood and effluent; the singing, screaming filth of pulped bodies, the choirs from within singing so sweetly, their songs of suffering more celebratory than the most evangelical hymn.

Down, into depths where every surface, every wall, floor and scrap of ceiling, flowed and dripped, where the countless forms strung and spitted, stitched or bound to the stone, writhing and shedding themselves, where those who hadn't ascended to the state of the angels practised their art, refined their faith, seeking fresh visions in the slitting of bellies, the stretching of skin, the plucking of nerve endings.

Down, down, through carpets of writhing, flayed flesh, through depths of meat and bone machinery; entire cloisters pulsing and whirring themselves to the point of dissolution, perpetually maintained by the engineers that scuttled and sweated there.

Down, through the states where the recently saved tumbled perpetually, pitched down flayed, naked and fraying apart by those that loved them more than any had in waking life, through flocks of metal and glass-winged birds, through swarms of crystalline butterflies, every inch fallen was a new exercise in mutilation, a new suite of experience, of transformation: a shuffling step closer to Nirvana.

Down, into the smoke-filled, lightning-wreathed darkness, the great workshops, where the birds and moths and engines were born; where the immense, serpentine conveyances he'd seen worming their way throughout the structure were partially cultivated, partially constructed, the process one part engineering to two biological gestation, the great, placental sacks in which they pulsed and swelled tended by numerous lesser engines, flayed and twitching midwives.

Here, she brought him to a halt, extending her hand so that he might see the work underway; industry the like of which would shame China,

Imperial Britain; tireless, ceaseless; souls running themselves to breaking and beyond, doing so happily, the overseers that drifted throughout needing no whips, no dogma or rhetoric to spur them; the suffering they endured more than sufficient threat and promise.

Many eyes were upon them, the work not stilling, even beneath the Inspirata's distraction, if anything, spurred into over-drive, those whose flesh failed; limbs tearing as they attempted to hoist some weight beyond their means, the circuits and devices grafted into their bodies sputtering, bursting with sheer exertion, others simply collapsing in the midst of their Sisyphian tasks, weeping in joy at their extremis.

The overseers were drifting, many-limbed entities, their frail bodies filleted, without weight or content, more subtle forms of machinery so deftly fused with their flesh, it was impossible to tell where it ended and anatomy began. At the end of every limb were devices, instruments; blades, welding implements… many whose purpose Sander couldn't even guess; fusions of what might be found in an industrial workshop and a surgical array, some beyond that; so strange and abstruse as to seemingly have no purpose. Each and every one of these boasted numerous eyes; permutations of the same device he bore, back in the flesh; that his Father had fashioned for him, though here in far more elaborate and advanced forms: their entire bodies fruiting with eyes like some bizarre, alien disease; an extra-dimensional cancer that caused the development of entire organs and systems, as opposed to merely knots of meaningless flesh, their natures as various as they were numerous; some slit and reptilian, others vast, fluttering; the eyes of innocents, of babes, of lovers… others resembling the machinery that seeded them; swivelling and telescoping arrays, hues of light cycling as they focussed and refocussed, seeking a more precise configuration.

It was an orchestrated dance, the overseers sifting around her like jellyfish, their attentions more piercing than knives, lashing and lancing him from myriad angles, sifting through the stuff of his life, his memory, with the same unthinking fascination, as though he were a frog on a biology student's desk, still writhing and kicking, despite having lost most of its entrails.

They loved him, singing to him; paternal and seducing, promising all he might be, all he might know, when he finally came to them in the flesh.

Not long, not long, now; his flesh calling, Fall's Edge already visible as a vague silhouette, shimmering before the sight that comprised him.

One broke from the shoal, abandoning its work, drawing closer than the rest, daring the Inspirata's fires, its eyes on him intense and familiar.

A voice, a name: 'Sander.'

Not like before; so far removed from the one that haunted memory, yet he knew from the first syllable: 'Dad?'

Laughter. 'Not any more. Or perhaps... more than ever.'

A bladed hand, extended to lightly caress, to rake through his lack of substance. He shuddered, knowing that he'd barely recall this on waking; that it would flitter and echo like something lost; a beloved memory; a childhood game, long since softened to sentiment.

'Beautiful. I knew you would be.'

'Let me be here. Let me stay with you.'

Laments, laughter, the creature's many eyes fluttering and weeping. 'I wish it could be that way, I truly do, my boy... but you still have work to do, so much work; so many eyes to open.'

Yes. The world still blind, no matter how many he bestowed eyes upon; how many scars he slit, how many tumours he surgically carved away... his fight a microcosm of that Abarise was built to wage: a war against human nature.

'There will be others, by and by; others who see, who know...they will help you, and you will help them.'

Yes, not like Nathaniel; little but an intruder in this story: others like the angel who bore him, like the children of Fall's Edge.

'They already sing your praises, Sander; the ones you have gifted, whose eyes you have opened. Listen! Can't you hear them?'

A cacophony, conflicting choruses, screams, whimpers; wordless pleas and prayers, the animal bleats of those reduced to little else, squirming and writhing in the muck of their mutilated selves, limbs shattered or sheared away, replaced by mechanisms or those of beasts... yes! Faint, distant; from somewhere far, far beyond these walls; his name, slurred and spat, vomited as though through throats full of living wasps and honey, in horror, in gratitude, in agony... rising up, from far, far below, sifting through the grated floor just as the filth of those pulped or spilled by their labours sluiced down; a place where they gathered, the eyeless seeing; where they suffered and saw so much more than he ever would in waking life...

Desperate, scrabbling in the angel's grip, even as it and Abarise faded around him, dispersing as though little more than a mirage; a confection of mist and smoke, a fever born hallucination...

'Please! Let me see them! Let me be with them!'

The thing that had been his Father ran its scalpel fingers through him, the promise of pain little comfort as all he'd ever wanted—the distorted Heaven he'd ached for every moment of his being—was denied.

They waited, as they had come at the angel's call. Nathaniel's hand was on Sander's shoulder, the heat and sourness of the man's breath coaxing him back towards waking.

Gone; the angel, her stories... where she'd taken him already ragged, sluicing away the more desperately he clutched and grasped.

A beautiful dream. A red dream.

Blazing heat, dust and thirst; the darkness behind his eyelids no defence, not since finding his Father's device. The engine inside stirred, writhing and weaving throughout, its tendrils simultaneously cold and burning, as though coated in frost.

'Sander.'

A soft summons, the man's rough hands smoothing the hair back from his sweat-beaded scalp. Something pressed to his lips... a plastic cup, cold water.

He drank, draining the fluid in an instant, pale light obliterating the world as his eyes snapped open, the vague, hazy silhouettes that inhabited it gathered and waiting; an audience to his disgrace.

'I think I know why we came here, now.'

Nathaniel, blue eyes wide as they roved over those gathered in the street: a rag-tag tribe of barely men and women; youths and adolescents, some hardly beyond childhood, wild-haired, wild-eyed, hands and faces smeared with dust, clothes torn and rumpled; seemingly scavenged from wherever they could find, some all but naked, their bruised and scarred bodies exposed to the sun and sand.

'Where...'

'Here, I think; from all over town. God knows how long they've been here.'

A flare of sunlight, a flux of shadows and darkness swelled before his enhanced eyes, creeping and flowing over the congregation, not masking or distorting their features, but *revealing* them; allowing him to peer beneath their masks of meat, to the state of their souls.

All like him; children of Abarise, come at the angel's call cast out by parental cruelty, the abuses of their towns, their schools, their churches. Come seeking, following dreams and visions across the desert.

Even the ones that never made it; the ghosts and shades, shoulder to shoulder with the living.

Nathaniel stood back, Sander wavered, barely able to hold himself upright.

'Hey! Where are you...'

Nathaniel grinned, placing his tattered, wide brimmed hat on his head.

'We're done, I think.'

An invisible knife in his gut, a hitched breath. 'Just like that?'

'Just like that. Unsatisfying, I know, but...' The man closed his eyes, brow furrowing, as though he heard something in the distance; something approaching fast. '...I've no more time to indulge myself. I was never really part of this, Sander; we both know it.'

Yes, from the start. He'd never made any secret of the fact. Even so, hearing it stated so bluntly hurt like a physical blow.

'...I probably should never have allowed it to go this far. I'm sorry for that, but...' Opening his eyes, casting them over the gathered crowd, more arriving from the town's outlying regions with every moment. '...I don't think you'll have much time to bemoan it.'

A crooked smile, a glimmer of sadness. For a moment, Sander was certain he had something else to say; some parting wit or revelation that hovered on his lips. Instead, he turned and paced back up the high street, into the dust and desert, leaving Sander in the company of his lost siblings.

They waited, these outcast children, waited for him to turn, to stagger their way, eyes never leaving him, as his never left them; the flickering, phantasmal beauty beyond their filth-smeared masks more than enough to exercise his fascination;

faces that many of them had never known before, outside of dreams, but that he would teach them to see, perhaps even to reveal, in time, as they would teach him to see and experience in ways not even his Father had dreamed of.

Going to them, he suffered their welcomes and embraces; the eyes and hands on him, their cannibal intimacy, as they carried him away, to the warrens where they might dream undisturbed, and wait for the day when the world no longer lamented seeing, or when it broke, and lost the means of denying its sighted children.

Without Fire
Ben Jacob

Jack was in trouble. And now, because Foster told me to check on Jack, I was too. I didn't even like Jack. He was the new guy in the pressing room. A big guy. Mangy. The moment I saw him I guessed he'd be trouble. The moment he started talking, I knew it.

All Jack talked about was Mini Worlds. The options, the extension kits, the stands, the day and night lights, the software, how to induce seasons—whether to induce seasons—what to do in case of famine, and on and on and on. I started to wish Weird Willy hadn't left. At least Willy's interest in homemade explosives had a practical dimension. I was *never* going to have a Mini World. Neither was Jack. A guy on the robot line could not own a Mini World. We'd never have the money, let alone the legal status. Jack might as well have been talking about getting a space ship. So we worked side by side picking the robot parts off the conveyer and boxing them, and stacking the boxes, and wrapping the boxes, and stacking the pallets of boxes among other palettes of boxes in the big storage room full of boxes. And Jack talked and talked about Mini Worlds and never stopped until the day he disappeared.

There's a rule at Robotek: three unauthorised days off in a year and you're out. On his fourth day, Jack was 'out'. That was when Foster asked if I knew where Jack lived. I didn't. It didn't matter.

'He hasn't responded to System Requests,' said Foster. 'Put this through his door.' Foster handed me a plastic card printed with the Robotek logo and uploaded Jack's name and address to my link. Jack Baker—the first time I knew his family name. I said 'Yes, Sir.' He said he'd replace Jack by the end of the week. I'd be on my own until then. It was Wednesday. Foster started out of the room.

'Sir,' I called. Foster paused. 'If that super-storm hits, do we get Friday off?'

'Check with the System,' said Foster and left.

I didn't go to Jack's that night. Robotek didn't pay extra to be a delivery boy. I went to Jack's the next day instead, after a shift at the pressing station alone.

Jack's place was close to mine in the Warrens, in a stack. The door to the entrance hall was open. The security scanners were broken. Tidal zones of litter and dust made patterns on the concrete floor. A chemical smell scraped at the twilight and half-masked the dull stench of dead things. A sign directed me to the stairs. I climbed them. Advertising announcements from outside echoed off the dirty walls. The walls had cracks from the last storm.

I didn't reach Jack's pod before I saw him. He was shuffling along the dim corridor ahead, wheezing like a rusty Mark Five, a heavy plastic six-litre bottle of water hanging from each arm. He greeted me, surprised.

'I've got an evaporation problem,' he said. I must have looked confused—I was confused. 'I'll show you.'

'That's okay.' I held out the Robotek card. 'The Boss asked me to drop this off.'

Jack's soft cheeks sagged.

'I'm out?'

I shrugged, thinking, of course you're out, you moron. Now, take it and let me get home.

He didn't take it. Without asking, he put the handle of one of the heavy bottles in my outstretched hand.

'I'll show you,' he said again.

'Look.' He had turned and was waddling along the corridor away from me, through the gloom, between the receding lines of pod doors. So, I'd help him with the bottle, that was reasonable—after all, the guy had just lost his job—then drop off the com-card and leave.

I caught up with Jack as he shouldered his way into the pod.

I said 'Here you are,' and put the heavy bottle inside the door. I produced the Robotek card again, which, again, he ignored.

'Wait,' he said. 'I haven't shown you.'

The twilight beyond Jack's big shape made me uneasy. A faint smell, not chemical, not rot, not unwelcoming, but unfamiliar, seeped from inside. That smell, more than Jack, made me curious to stay just long enough to see what it was.

Light in the pod came from one bright source, but it wasn't a screen. As I drifted cautiously in I saw the screen was off, I don't think I'd ever been in a pod with the screen off—or one so empty of possessions.

The source of light was a large, open-topped box, a metre and a half square and fifty centimetres high, balanced on the counter that separated the kitchen from the living-sleeping space. A tangle of black umbilical cables emerged from it and entered a socket on the wall next to a meal-maker that, even in the gloom, displayed a shell-like crust of burnt food. More slops and stains were evident around the kitchen, but, like the rest of the pod they were shadowy ornamentations. My attention was drawn to the box on the counter above which a small, bright light shone.

'That's it,' whispered Jack.

I drifted towards it, my leg brushing something unnoticed in the gloom. It felt and sounded like a large, empty box.

'Sorry,' muttered Jack. 'I haven't thrown out the packing. The delivery guys said this was the only time they'd delivered to the Warrens. They always go to the Villas.'

Of course they do, I was thinking, if it's what I think it is, it costs a fortune. Thoughts of money, the rest of the pod, the Warrens and Robotek faded the moment I looked into the box.

In the box was a very small island.

The island was about the size and shape of the orange helmets worn at the factory. Domed and vaguely oval, its minute shores of rock and sand were lapped by the tiny waves of a sea contained inside the box. The 'sea' was perhaps 15 centimetres deep, which made it nearly twice as deep as the island was tall. The inner walls of the container were coloured pale blue, deepening towards the upper rim. From the island there might have been the illusion of infinite sky. Around the shoreline of the island ran a slim ring of sand. Along the sand tiny palm trees shook emerald fronds in the faintest of breezes. Each tree was no taller than the first joint of my little finger. Among them were a few wooden houses each a centimetre or two long and shorter than the palm trees. I'd seen holo-tisements for Mini Worlds, but it was only in that moment that I understood their magic. I didn't just understand it. I felt it. That tiny world was so detailed, intricate, precious.

Along one of the strips of sand moved a few tiny coloured shapes, like small ants walking upright.

'Don't breathe on it,' hissed Jack, quickly. I was holding my breath anyway. 'What do you think?'

It was beautiful. A living gem.

'I have ten people,' said Jack, quietly. 'You can see some there, on the beach. They say you should keep the ratios fifty-fifty, so there are five couples. Each one is genetically differentiated. Perfect, just like you and me, but one two-hundred-and-thirtieth of the size.'

I watched the moving ant-people. I wanted to laugh, but it felt wrong. I wanted to cry, but that felt wrong too. I couldn't hold my breath any longer. I straightened, breathing out in a burst.

'Amazing.' I whispered.

'They can do everything we can.'

'They shit?'

Jack's big head bobbed.

'The water absorbs their waste and gets filtered. The City Mini Worlds have working sewerage system, but this one's all I could afford. It's based on those flooded South Pacific islands.'

'Can they... have babies?'

'You need the right conditions, but...'

'They can have babies *naturally*?'

'Sure: no sperm banks, no application process, no licences. But it's risky. Some of the females could die. And the children. They only have what they can make from materials on the island. There are no medicines. No hospital. It's basically us, two thousand years ago. That's why you can't breathe on it. They're immune to all common and hereditary diseases, but you never quite know what can happen at that level of life. Aerosols for example, are a big no-no. Each molecule is huge to those little guys.'

Like a diver in an old documentary, I sucked in the biggest lungful of Jack's stale pod air and realised what that alien, but welcoming aroma was. It was coming from the island. The smell of life. I stooped closer. I wanted to take it all in. I wanted to see the people. They seemed to be exploring, gathering, organising.

'Don't get under the light!' said Jack, his fat hand on my shoulder. 'Stay above the light. Eclipses freak them out.'

A narrow, clear, plastic arch spanned the 'sky' above the box. A little section of it emitted bright light onto the island.

'That's the sun-arch,' explained Jack. 'Aside from people I got six goats and some chickens. I really wanted a tiger, but thought it'd kill the goats and then start going after the people. You have to be really careful which animals you put together.'

'What do they eat?'

Jack explained the islanders didn't have fire but they had genetically miniaturised carrots, coconuts, lettuces, and bananas, which grew in real organic, purified soil—it cost a fortune per bag. He told me how each person lived for around four hundred and fifty of our days and how one day for them was twenty-four of our minutes.

'They don't live long.' I watched a tiny person attempting to herd goats between the palm trees. The 'sun' was getting low in the 'sky'. The people were gathering around their huts.

'If the conditions are right they'll have children,' explained Jack, watching the light fading to darkness with satisfaction, like a fleshy idol, 'so you can have younger generations and they won't die out.'

'What if you get too many children?'

'You can sell them. That's what I want to do: give them perfect conditions, let them breed, sell the young ones. It's an investment.'

'Won't they get freaked out if your hand appears from the sky and starts carrying off their children?'

'There's a gas. A little canister. You use it any time you have to interfere. The gas sends them to sleep for a couple of hours—

our time, not theirs.'

I gulped in more air and stooped back low to watch. The light was too dim and the people were too small to make out individual features, but you could see them facing one another—talking, I supposed. I straightened again to breathe.

'Do they know we are here?'

'They have a sense of another presence, but they don't know what that is. I mean, they are capable of evolving and exploration, logic and reasoning, so there's a chance that one day they will try and cross the sea, reach the wall and create their own cosmology based on that. Some guys on the forums have done experiments—they take some of the population out, let them experience the outer world, then put them back in. It never goes well. They die or are rejected by the rest of the population.' Jack shook his head. 'I don't know why anyone'd want to piss around with them like that. If nothing else you'd be destroying thousands of bits worth of stuff—but then, a lot of the people who own these have more bits than sense. Guess how much each person costs?'

'A thousand?'

'Three.'

'Three thousand bits? That's... impossible.' It was like he had taken my brain and slapped it.

'That's without the island, the weather-matic, the wave-matic, the sun-arch. I had to bribe people too.' He shrugged. 'Technically it's restricted goods. It cost tens of thousands.'

'How did you...?'

'Savings,' he said. 'Sold everything else. This is all I want. I borrowed the rest—most of it, actually.'

'Who from?' I recalled the Robotek card. Jack wasn't going back to Robotek. The weekly repayments on tens of thousands would be crippling.

'Do you mind?' He ignored my question.

I shuffled to one side as he hauled one of the water bottles up to the counter. From a plastic bag he took a blue sachet and a narrow metal spatula. Holding the delicate tool in his fat fingers, he transferred two small heaps of blue powder from the sachet and emptied them into the neck of the bottle, replaced the bottle top, shook it then opened it and poured the water into the tank, carefully directing it so that it ran down the sides of the Mini World's sky-walls without causing a splash. The sea level rose. A few tiny people on the twilit beach watched the tide come in. Some let it reach their legs, others retreated to high ground.

I wanted to remain under the spell of the island, but I felt uncomfortable having to deliver Foster's message. I put the Robotek card on Jack's kitchen counter away from the light of the Mini World, made my excuses and left.

That night my pod screen flashed with warnings of the storm approaching beyond the dome. It showed images of gate guards shooting Warren residents who wanted to reach the refuges. I watched and failed to sleep, but not from concern about the storm. It was as if something had detached me from those events and that thing floated in my thoughts like a fond memory of life I had never had but to which I wanted to return. Those memories were of an emerald island in a tiny sea, where food grew in unpolluted earth and the tide rose over people's legs, where there was no fire and no storms.

The next morning the System didn't say anything about a storm closure at Robotek. That didn't mean I went to work. I'd discovered something more valuable. I hardly noticed the Warren's foetid air, dense with the clamour of sirens and warnings as I made my way back to Jack's.

Jack was slow to open the door. It wasn't just that he wasn't expecting me, he didn't want to open it. Through the cracked door unit he asked who I was, why I was there, who sent me. I told him no one sent me, I wanted to see the island. He said he felt ill. I said I could look after him. He said he was tired. I said he could rest if he wanted. Maybe he was angry at me for delivering the com-card. If it wasn't for the persistent feeling that I needed to see that tiny world, I might have given up and gone to work.

'Is anyone else with you?' Jack asked in the end.

'No.'

The gloomy corridor was empty. Most people from the Warrens were trying to reach the refuges.

The door slid open. Jack stuck his fat head out. I saw him and winced. Blood had leaked from cuts and dried in dark lines around his lips. One cheek looked ready to hatch a creature of blood. His right eye was a weeping crack. His left eye quickly checked the corridor.

'What happened?'

He stepped aside, urgently ushering me in. I squeezed past. Jack locked the door. We were surrounded again by gloom. It was easier to face Jack in the dimness.

'The collectors visited.'

'You should go to a clinic.'

'And let them take this away?' He stabbed a fat fist at the glowing box on the kitchen counter. It was comforting, the way it spilled light and the faint aroma of life, weather-matics and wave-matics whirring softly. I was relieved nothing had happened to it. 'They said they'd come back.'

'How much do you need?' We were whispering.

'Three thousand.' You had to borrow a lot to get a first repayment of three thousand. A lot. Jack blinked at me. 'I don't have it.'

Of course he didn't. His swollen cheeks and eyes drooped.

'I can look after the island,' I said, 'while you go to the clinic.'

'And if they come back?'

'I'll call security.'

'No!' He held up both fat palms to say 'stop'. 'You can't call security. They'll see I have restricted goods.' Jack shook his head. 'Even if they don't come, something might go wrong while I'm out. The weather-matic could overheat or... they might start a rebellion or... there's too much you don't know.'

'We could move it to mine.'

Again, Jack shook his fat, broken head.

'Once it's activated, you can't. The trauma a world experiences when it's moved is irreversible. The chickens might survive and the plants, but the people?'

'Send them to sleep with that special gas.'

'I've run out.'

'So get some more.'

'How?'

He was right. We didn't have the right status and now he didn't have any money.

'How about I get you something for your cuts? I've got stuff at mine.'

'You'd do that?'

'Sure,' I said, my attention drifting to the light of the sun-arch low in the box over the island. 'For them.'

Jack's fat face creased into a smile.

'Can I take a look before I go?'

As I stepped past, drawn to the glow, Jack made an unexpected lunge at something. He slammed the sole of one boot onto the floor. Startled, I glimpsed a small, sleek, multi-legged black shape scuttle for cover.

'Shit,' muttered Jack.

'You should spray the place.'

'It'd ruin the world. The concentrations of a spray would be enormous for them. They could die.'

'But what if a roach gets in there?'

'It can't.' Jack's good eye was a big circle. 'That can't happen. Any insects, anything like that, they'd be monsters. You have to be very careful. There's a cover you can get—Crystal Dome 180—but it doesn't come supplied. I got the weather-matic instead. The dome stops dust and organic intruders, but it obscures the view and air flow...' He trailed off, looking at the Mini World. 'You can get condensation on the inside too.'

I had an image of tiny people battling a monstrous insect with sticks. I guessed there was no metal on the island—they could never evolve into making machines. I recalled the Robotek pressing room, the relentless slamming of the machines, metal on metal making robot parts. My heart beat faster, roused by the palm fronds trembling in the sea breeze to the faint sound of minute waves. I wanted to be on that island, my tiny feet on organic earth. A wife. A hut. Children.

Five minutes later I dragged myself away. I'd be back soon. Jack locked the door. I hurried home.

The Warren walkways were clogged with guards and crowds. The Warrens were designed to protect us from the storms until the dome was complete, but if the wind came from a particular direction it swept over the walls of the dome and was funnelled down the alleys where it gathered dust, ash and litter and flung it around with a roar. Men and women hunched against the wind. Loudspeakers warned everyone to stay inside, but all I heard from the people I passed was that the dome could not stand another storm. It took longer than I thought to reach my pod.

The screen came on as I entered. It showed a newscaster saying that contact had been lost with the Americas. She said air traffic was grounded. She said to expect loss of power. As she talked, images flashed on the screen of armed robots deployed beneath the dome. I recognized their body parts. I wanted to get away from those crowds, the wind, the robots, back to the island to protect that little paradise.

I grabbed a bag and threw in useful things: water, food capsules, portable LED, bandages, painkillers. Shouldering my baseball bat and the bag, I set the door to lock behind me.

You can't go running through the Warrens with a baseball bat, not with so many guards around, so it took me longer than I thought, ducking from doorway to doorway, waiting for troops to pass, battling against the surge of worried faces who were pressing the other way, before, breathless, I reached Jack's.

The door to Jack's was open.

An ominous red cipher glistened on the dusty threshold. Red droplets continued the message up the corridor to the higher levels. I didn't follow them. I guessed the story they told—but was it Jack's or a collector's?

I stopped at the door, shifted the bat to my stronger arm ready to swing. My throat felt narrow and dry.

'Hello?' I called.

No reply.

I edged inside. Called again.

No reply. Nothing moved. Maybe Jack was fine. Maybe one of his cuts had opened and he had gone to get some water and left the door open for my return.

My weak shadow fell on a clutter of ashen shapes and flowed on, merging with darkness, darkness unbroken by any tiny artificial sun. The island was gone.

In that moment the darkness of the pod threatened to tumble into me. I held it at bay with the thought that maybe it was night in the Mini World and its sun would rise again in a few minutes. I scrabbled around, trying to activate the light sensors. Maybe they were broken. Maybe the power had been lost and that was why the Mini World had no glow. Would the island survive without power? Would the mini people be panicking at the loss of their sun? Maybe the LED in my bag could work instead.

Dropping the bat, I crouched, opened the bag, working by touch, found the little diode. I pulled it out, switched it on and swept its beam across the pod.

Jack wasn't there.

The Mini World was. Sort of. Someone had ripped the cables out, tipped it off the counter and kicked it, stamped on it, broke it. The container and the sun-arch were mangled, the island hidden in a puddle of water. A small, sleek black shape was brooding on the edge of the pool. I crept in horror towards the ruined world, towards the little creature. The insect skittered reluctantly into the shadows but left something small behind. I stooped closer.

Limp, headless, like a drowned ant with two arms, two legs, a tiny naked body lay there. Others were scattered in what had been the sea, now a pool of salty water on a dirty floor. On hands and knees I approached the upturned world. Then I saw them.

Two tiny people were clinging to each other, up to their knees in water.

Holding my breath so it didn't knock them over, I lowered my face to the floor, let the diode shine on them, the last survivors. A tiny man holding a tiny woman.

I grabbed a strip of broken plastic, perhaps part of the Mini World box, off the floor and holding one end, offered it to them as a raft. The man struggled onto it, carrying the woman.

Cupping one hand underneath, gently, slowly, I raised them from the ground. Kneeling, I held them up to my eye. The little man was sagging, weak. The woman lay unmoving at his feet.

The little man's bowed shoulders straightened. He looked at me. With tiny arms he gestured. He was shouting, angry, frightened, but I couldn't hear him. Who am I to him, I wondered, knowing what I must do. A god? A monster?

Then the sad wail of the storm sirens rose on the strengthening wind.

In the Stationary Cupboard
Greg Michaelson

I was denounced at the National Convention. Although an elected representative, I was suspended from my post the next morning and arrested that afternoon. The warrant charged me with breaching laws that I had helped frame: 'Behaviour incompatible with social cohesion.' My trial was cursory, if formally correct, and I was sentenced to a term in the camp in the far north-west. Once I would have been crushed and humiliated: I had pledged myself to freeing our country and the Party had been my lifeblood. Now, I really didn't care.

Immediately after the trial, I was taken to the station and put on the train north. There was no point in trying to flee; I was continuously tracked by the electronic tag on my left ankle. Besides, as a prominent former member of the Committee of National Reconstruction, I was well known and better disliked. On the train, my fellow travellers shunned me.

Aloof, I huddled by the window, idly watching the deer grazing the high flanks of the glens. Twenty years before, we had hidden on these hills from the helicopter gun-ships. Then, we were heroes, liberators, brave hearts.

At the port, the sea was rough and the ferry to the island was delayed. I was cold and hungry; I hadn't eaten since we'd left the city. On the quay, there was a small kiosk, run by a frail woman with long grey hair. It sold sandwiches and hot drinks, but I had no money. I walked out onto the harbour wall. Watching the waves break on the mole, I mused on how our hopes had shattered on expediency.

Clara and I had come here years ago, long before the uprising. Staring across the Minch, I remembered twilight walks along the strand at low tide, skimming stones and arguing affectionately. I had dreamed of a simpler yet richer life, of comradeship and cheer. She was hard and practical, mocking my romantic sensibilities.

I had last seen her in the basement of the Central Police Station, slumped in a pool of blood and excrement. My memory of her torment sustained me throughout our struggle. After Liberation, they carved her name on the Martyrs Monument.

A quiet voice behind me said, 'Excuse me.'

I turned to find the woman from the kiosk proffering me a cup of tea. I thanked her profusely and drank it down. Instead of leaving, she watched expectantly, as if we had unfinished business.

'You don't remember me, do you' she said finally, and swept the hair back from her forehead.

I started, and stared in recognition at the white scar above her left eye.

'Of course I remember you,' I said. 'What are you doing here? I thought they'd freed you years ago.'

'I'd nothing to go back to,' she said. 'So I stayed. No one knows me here any longer. I feel like Pirate Jenny, watching the boats come and go.'

'You should have come and found me,' I said.

'Should I?' she said, softly. 'Should I?'

'I'm sorry,' I said, sadly. 'What else could I have done.'

'Nothing, I expected nothing else. Were I you, I'd have done the same. But I can't forget. And I don't want to.'

'Aye well,' I said. 'Now it's my turn.'

I drained the tea and handed her the cup. As she reached over to take it from me, I was shocked to see jagged, angry welts on her wrist.

'Did they do that to you,' I asked. 'I thought at least we'd stopped all that.'

'No,' she said, quickly tugging down her coat sleeve and taking the cup. 'It wasn't them.'

'Is it really that bad over there?' I was aghast that someone so strong and stubborn should try to kill themself.

'You'll see,' she said. 'Let me give you some advice. Keep out of the stationary cupboard.'

'The stationary cupboard?'

'That's right,' she said, turning back to the kiosk.

'Will you still be here when I get out?' I persisted.

'I'm not going anywhere.' She walked back down the mole. 'Et in Arcadia ego.'

The ferry docked and they herded us onboard. The crossing was choppy. I was glad to step ashore. From the docks, we walked in a column across the town to the main gate where we were strip-searched. Beyond the gate, on the road to the reception centre, we met a team of inmates in grey uniforms, cutting peats.

The reception centre was housed in the old post office behind the standing stones. I was strip searched again, given an ill-fitting uniform and allocated to a room in a dormitory block in a former construction yard. I was also issued with a minimum ration credit card. Work was optional for social prisoners, but life on minimum rations was meagre. I asked for an office job and tried to tell them about my qualifications and skills. They laughed and said that there were only placements in the wind generator factory or the fields: I spent the first winter at a bench, bolting blades onto drive shafts.

I'd had pleurisy as a child and my lungs had never fully recovered. The factory was poorly heated and damp. Early in the New Year, I came down with pneumonia. Running a high fever, I collapsed and was sent to the prison hospital. For four days I lay in bed, soaked in sweat and racked with crazed visions. One dream kept coming back, stronger and stronger, until it crowded out the others.

We were running through the bracken, unarmed and naked, under the blazing midday sun, pursued by vast tracked leviathans. One by one, my companions were cut down by steel bolts from the steam-powered crossbows mounted on the behemoths' stone hulls. At first I woke screaming as each comrade fell, but as the dream repeated I ran further and further across the moors. At last, at the base of what seemed like a gentle rise, I looked back to find I was the only one of our group still alive. The leviathans gained on me, but as the rise grew steeper my pace grew stronger. As I neared the crest I turned back again: the cruel machines were floundering and, one by one, toppled over.

I crossed the rise and walked down the hill to the sea. A small dinghy was moored just off shore. I waded out through the surf, hoisted the sail and guided the boat across the straits to the island. Landfall: I dragged the boat through the surf and up the strand. Crossing the dunes, a grassy plain opened out in front of me. In the centre of the plain was the megalith, the cruciform aisles of freshly dressed stone glistening in the sunlight. As I approached the woman in the centre of the circle, she stood and turned and held out her arms to me. Overcome with joy, I ran through the stones towards her.

And sat bolt upright, exhausted, my fever gone.

I made a slow recovery: my lungs took several months to heal fully. There was a small library in the hospital and I spent most of my days lying on my back reading.

Every night, my dream recurred, becoming more and more vivid and detailed. As my dream grew, Clara steadily led me from the stones to a small community of white houses by the loch, populated by my dead family and friends, living that utopia she had taught me to despise.

On discharge, I was deemed unfit for further manual labour. The hospital library was disorganised, with no central catalogue or lending system, so I offered to run it in exchange for a hot meal once a day. They found me an ageing computer and I began to leisurely, but systematically, type details of all the books into a simple spreadsheet. When I had populated the spreadsheet, I started another to record loans.

During the days, as I typed, I found myself musing on my dream. I was plainly not dead and yet I could visit the dead. Clara was central to my dream. Perhaps I was Dante to her Beatrice, but she offered me no transcendent visions of perfection. Perhaps I was Orpheus to her Eurydice, but she had no wish to leave.

When the hospital library system was up and running, I had little to do. In the spring, I told the hospital managers that I was going to request a fresh work allocation, but they asked me to stay on as a clerk. My job involved maintaining the medical records and taking the updates to the reception centre. I enjoyed my relative freedom of movement, but was still deeply lonely and isolated.

My dream began to change subtly. The more often I visited the village beyond the stones, the more complex the people grew, as if my memory was reconstructing them in greater and greater detail.

One night, Clara, who was becoming curiously argumentative, asked me why I kept leaving. Nonplussed, I told her that I wasn't dead. She called me a silkie and became morose. I protested and asked her what she meant. She said that the living eventually grew tired of the lack of change beyond death. I asked her how I could stay. She baldly told me that first I'd have to die.

I awoke feeling deeply disturbed. Despite my privations, I wasn't planning on dying for a good while yet. I knew I could face death for those I loved and a cause I cherished, but to actively kill myself was unthinkable.

The next night, my sleep was dreamless. The dream never returned.

On a grey autumn day, I was told to collect office supplies. The reception centre was out of bounds for most prisoners so I handed in a requisition at the front desk and was asked to wait outside the store for the order to be made up.

The store was guarded by a huge mastiff that barked menacingly as I approached. I kept my distance and stood in the drizzle, watching the door.

When the storekeeper emerged I was surprised to find that I knew him. A former member of my unit, he had been wounded in an ambush during our flight in the heather and I had helped carry him to safety. After Liberation, he had opposed the incorporation of our partisans into the regular army and became one of the first camp inmates. I learnt later that, although long freed, he had chosen to stay behind, like the woman on the quayside.

The storekeeper calmed the dog and greeted me warmly.

'You old bastard!' he said. 'I'd heard you were here. How things change, eh? You'd better come in.'

'Is it safe?' I asked.

'Oh yes,' he said. 'No one'll bother us.'

The storekeeper ushered me into the store.

'You'll be looking for the stationary cupboard. It's that way.'

He pointed down a row of deep metal racking. As the right sleeve of his stained brown overalls rolled up his arm, I noticed the livid purple gouges across his wrist, and remembered the woman on the jetty.

'What are you gawping at?' said the storekeeper.

He picked up an old magazine and read.

At the end of the shelves, on the far wall, was a door with 'Stationary Cupboard' crudely stencilled across it. Pinned above the stencil was a postcard of a plaque carved with a stone tank traversing a wooded landscape. Below the tank was the caption: 'ET IN ARCADIA EGO/After Nicolas Poussin'.

Then I remembered the parting words of the woman on the quay. Was I being mocked? Had I come to yet another dead end?

Looking round, I noticed that there were windows on either side of the door. Peering through the left hand window, all I could see was the gloomy deserted yard. If the door led anywhere it was back outside, and was bound to be heavily bolted.

'Out you go!' called the storekeeper from the other end of the building.

Feeling foolish, I tried the door handle. The handle turned, the door opened, and I started as I looked out, across an enclosed paved courtyard, at a worn flight of stone steps which led up and away into bright sunlight.

'Shut the bloody door!' shouted the storekeeper.

I stepped into the courtyard, pulled the door behind me and mounted the stairs. At the top, a grassy plain opened out in front of me. In the centre of the plain was the megalith, the cruciform aisles of freshly dressed stone glistening in the sunlight. As I approached the woman in the centre of the circle, she stood and turned and held out her arms. Overcome with joy, I ran through the stones towards her. Silently, she took me by the hands and led me down the hill to the white-washed village by the loch.

I had not realised how much I had longed for release from the loathsome drudgery of my former life. But I had no awareness of having died.

I quickly settled into my new existence. I learnt to fish and plough, to cut peat and milk goats. The seasons came and went, and the land and sea were always fertile. Every day was orderly without being ordered. We danced and ate and made love and sang and cooked and told stories and sat quietly just being with each other. The years flew past.

But somehow it wasn't enough. I couldn't forget the world I'd left behind, how hard we'd fought to better it, and how much harder we should have fought to make it better. In stark contrast, nobody here was concerned with what had been. For them, there was no way back, and their one certainty was that everyone they'd left behind must eventually join them.

As I grew used to this strangely familiar other life, I realised more and more how Clara had changed from the comrade I'd mourned so long: the Clara, whose bitter death yet haunted me, who'd scorned this bucolic utopia.

But whenever I tried to discuss this with Clara, she looked sad, and then laughed and told me how much better off I was now. But despite her comfort I became increasingly morose, and took to spending time alone, musing on what might have been.

Late one afternoon, I was up on the hill gathering sheep's wool from the brambles. It was a cloudy day, but as I turned for home the sun broke through and lit up the standing stones. The dancing shadows called to me so I shouldered my pack and set off up the hill.

As I neared the megalith, I tripped on a root and fell forward into the heather. As I picked myself up, I noticed a rectangular rock jutting from the scrub. The rock was unnaturally smooth. I cleared away the heather obscuring its face. The rock was carved with a stone tank traversing a wooded landscape. Below the tank was the caption: 'ET IN ARCADIA EGO/After Nicolas Poussin'.

It was my turn to laugh: the past had returned to mock me. I was not dead, but my living dream was a pale pastiche of my waking hopes. The plaque was not very large. Perhaps I could take it back to the village as a *momento vita*.

As I bent over and hefted the rock, the ground parted revealing a worn flight of stone steps leading down to an enclosed paved courtyard. I felt my life calling to me. In a daze, I went down the steps into the courtyard and found myself back outside the door to the store. So many years had gone by. Surely the camp wasn't still here. It couldn't hurt to check.

I opened the door and stepped into the shed. As the door closed loudly behind me, the storekeeper looked up from his magazine.

'Back already?' he asked. 'I'd better get your stocks then.'

Nothing had changed. No time had passed. I panicked and desperately pulled at the door, which opened onto the gloomy deserted yard.

'There's no escape,' said the storekeeper, scratching at his wrist, a crazed glint in his eyes. 'I've tried, believe me. Here's your stuff. You better be off then.'

He ushered me out of the building. The dog growled as I set off through the rain back to the hospital.

The Floating Market
Sonya Blanck

The sun beat down on the dry prairie grass. She took a breath from her oxivape. The end of the dry season would come soon—but not soon enough.

The settlement had three days' worth of dry goods, maybe a week of tinned preserves. The leathery fruit jerky and wheat meat was gone, and half the grain had spoiled. The floating market had left the shallow river, and the clams had to be left to replenish their numbers. They had nothing to trade for beans.

The most able had drawn dry straws of hay to see who would carry the stain of killing on their soul, and Amy'd got the shortest. The Elder took her into the dusty temple's sacred heart, placed the polished quartz diode round her wrinkled neck into a finely-calibrated hole in the ground, and retrieved the dreaded instrument from a trapdoor.

The Elder's eyes were bright and heavy as she placed the laser cannon into Amy's hands. Its size was belied by its weight, and she nearly dropped it for shaking.

'This hasn't been seen since I was young. Honour the life you steal.'

Amy pocketed the vape, no longer feeling dizzy. A young doe approached her, unafraid. Her hide was dull, but yes, she still had some meat on her. The doe came closer, perhaps to nuzzle her legs. She trembled as she raised the cannon.

From deeply-buried instinct, the doe stopped, the guide laser wavering on her forehead. Then, without feeling it, she squeezed the trigger before the doe could run. The animal instantly sank inert, falling over onto her side.

Amy ran to the doe, hot viscous tears pricking her eyes, and bent over the still-warm body. *'I'm sorry,'* she whispered close to the lifeless face as her own twisted with sobs. *'I'm sorry.'*

Monsoon season had come to the Lund archipelago, and brought its pervasive damp to baked ground parched from months of drought. Consequently, the River Tamys was higher than usual, an unwelcome guest in the cellar of Stef's house in the Croft.

Wonderful, she thought.

Stef had planned for this contingency long ago by stripping away the carpet, and keeping her valuable wares in watertight boxes. She would be prepared, even if the Elders weren't.

But she didn't like the look of the six inches of water eddying around her goods on the cellar floor. *Time to get some flood boards.*

Wellies on, she grabbed her kayak and oar from the teeming garden and stepped out her side gate, only a few feet above the encroaching bank. Her gaze lingered on the current, which was overgorged and sluggish. She felt momentarily dizzy and, leaning her transportation against a pebbledash wall, nipped inside to grab her oxivape, taking a long pull for the journey ahead before stowing it in her stuffed bag.

Where to trade today? She normally parked at the Spike, but tethers came dear, and all she wanted was to pass through, hopefully gaining flood boards in the process. She aimed instead at the Summit, gliding lazily through the current until she could see the glass of its peak looming before her, surrounded by a varied fleet of vessels.

Stef weaved through the tethers, past narrowboats hawking their wares, until she arrived at the deck of a black boat stacked high with PVC guards. The tattooed captain flashed a gaptoothed smile as she tied up her kayak and stepped aboard.

'Need some caulking help? I accept, ah, other forms of payment,' he winked.

'I keep pay and fun separate,' she giggled as she unzipped her bag, heaving with dry beans.

I found a pearl in my oyster, last night. I found it while I was shucking a bucket for dinner. It was there when I cracked open the shell, smooth and pale, like a shiny dried soya bean.

I showed it to Mumma as she tended the vegetables on the stove. Her eyes widened, then sunk dolefully back down to her pan. 'You could trade that for a fair few beans tomorrow,' she said. I thought she would be happy, and I told her so.

Her back straightened a little. 'I *am* happy for you,' she said. 'I just wish…'

'What?'

'I wish the world would let you keep it.'

They don't trade pearls at the local floating market—nobody has much use for beauty, in my neighbourhood—so this morning I borrowed the kayak and paddled it downstream until I got to the Islands, jutting their ruined metal and water-carved glass into the sky. I passed the Spike, where a rainbow of boats and buoys bobbed in the current, and I knew I couldn't trade it there. I saw a riot of boat food, plants, sandbags—nothing beautiful, for beauty's sake.

But then I saw you, milady, draped in your fine linen with glittering jewels in each ear, proudly piloting your silent canoe, and I knew that emissaries like you were a home for beauty in this world.

So, take my pearl. I won't ask for too many beans. I know you can't pass light through it, or wire it into the brainmesh your people weave. But it is fine in its own way. How grand, that an oyster's irritation can produce this iridescent little tear. It would fit beautifully into your necklace.

Please, take the beauty of my land, and honour it. Honour the life you steal.

By Herself
Fiona Ashley

Olivia stood at the kitchen window and looked out for the papergirl. She liked looking out. The street was pleasant, all the gardens were neat and the hedges free from rubbish. She soon saw the girl on her bicycle. 'Tuesday again, Mrs McLeod,' she said cheerily.

'Aye lass, Tuesday again,' smiled Olivia. Tuesday was the one day she was certain of. Tuesday was her magazine day.

She made herself a pot of tea, arranged it on a tray, then carried it out to the front door. She struggled to know what to call the front of the house in this lovely neighbourhood. She always just called it 'the front' before. *I'm going to take my tea at the front. It's lovely at the front today, come and sit with me.* But the front here seemed to demand a name—the porch or the veranda.

She sat on her wicker chair and opened her favourite magazine, 'The Woman's Companion'. The first story was called 'The Package Holiday', it was about a young lassie on holiday with her two bairns, but the lassie was not enjoying herself. She only brightened up at the end when one of the bairns announced that this was the best holiday—ever! Olivia was bothered by the story. She couldn't quite put her finger on it. The lassie in the story had no right to be so miserable. She had a lovely holiday and two happy bairns. Maybe they were a lot of work and she was by herself, but that was no reason to complain.

She put her cup down carefully as an idea occurred to her. She said it out loud, 'She's by herself,' verbalising the thought to keep it from disappearing. Olivia glimpsed a shadow of a memory, just materialising. She waited for it to solidify into something more substantial. She's by herself.

Olivia looked over to Mrs MacDonald's house across the road, hoping to see her neighbour sitting on her kitchen chair, carried out to the front for a bit of sunshine. She crossed the road. 'Lovely day today, Olivia,' Mrs MacDonald greeted her.

'Ruby,' she hesitated, not sure how to explain her thinking, 'why are all the women on their own here?'

Mrs MacDonald looked puzzled, glancing up and down the street as if to confirm what Olivia said. 'I've no idea,' she said eventually. 'I know my man liked a drink before he got handy with his fists, so I've no desire to have him here. What about your man?'

'I don't know,' replied Olivia. 'Before today I had no thoughts about him at all, like he never existed.'

She felt the idea of a husband in her head, but no more than an outline, she couldn't remember his name, the colour of his eyes, nothing. But she had a very strong sense he had been with her before here.

The Registry was a huge building and the front door was a revolving one, making everyone hesitate before they went in. Olivia broke her step and nearly lost her nerve, but she allowed herself to be swallowed up by the door and spat out the other side. She sorted her coat and straightened her hat before she approached the middle-aged woman who sat behind the reception desk. She was formally dressed in a navy suit with a light blue blouse.

'Hello, welcome to the Registry. What can I help you with today?'

Olivia felt herself tense. 'I've come to find out about my man. I don't know why I haven't done it before, but I only just remembered him.' Her words tumbled out like they were afraid to wait.

Navy suit smiled, 'Let me get someone to help you.' She pressed a button on the desk and a young lassie appeared from the glass doors behind her. 'Jess, can you help Mrs MacLeod with her query, please?' she asked.

'No problem,' Jess replied. They walked over to the lifts and waited for one to reach reception. 'I'm Jess,' the lassie said, 'I'm going to take you to the library to start our search. Everything you need will be in the library.'

The lift doors opened into a room, the like of which Olivia had never seen before. There were rows and rows of shelves, stretching further than she could see, and each shelf was covered in books, all shapes, colours and sizes. The shelves reached up to the roof and there were huge wooden ladders attached on rails. Folk were sliding them along before climbing up and taking a book down, then moving it to another shelf. Olivia marvelled how they could ever find anything. Jess touched her lightly on the arm, 'Come on, let's go and sit down.' She lead Olivia to a series of desks of heavy dark wood with reading lights on top. Olivia perched on the edge of a wooden chair with red velvet upholstery. 'I've never seen anything like this before,' she confided in Jess.

She nodded. 'Everyone says that.'

Olivia finished her request and waited. 'Mrs MacLeod,' Jess began, 'I can get you answers but you have to understand that they might not be the answers you want. The library contains all the books we'll need, but you have no control over what the books say.'

'I don't understand,' said Olivia, 'how can books tell me about my man? Was he famous? Did he do something worth writing about?'

Jess smiled, 'Everyone is worth writing about, Mrs MacLeod, that's what this library is all about. Everyone has their own book, about themselves, kept in this library. New books are started every day and old ones are archived. Now, I don't know if your husband is still current or if he's been archived, that's the first thing I have to check. But you must understand,' she hesitated, 'books tell the truth about a person, no showing your best side here. If we find his book, you have to accept what it says. Are you sure you want me to look for it?'

Olivia bristled, 'You're making me think my man did something wrong!'

'We've all done something wrong, Mrs MacLeod,' Jess smiled again. 'Now, some tea for you, I think, this search might take a while.'

Her tea was finished when Jess came back. She was carrying a green book, quite small book with a soft leather cover.

'Is that it?' asked Olivia.

'No,' said Jess. 'Your man's book is in the restricted section. I can't let you see it, I'm afraid.'

A tickle of fear ran over Olivia's skin. 'Why is it restricted?'

Jess laid her hand over Olivia's. 'Everyone's story involves other people, the people they interact with, the people they are married to, the people they chat to on the bus. This means that other people have some say over who gets to read about them, even if they are written down in your book. If the other person is still writing their own book, then archived books that they appear in can be restricted.'

Olivia licked her lips anxiously, 'So it's not necessarily a bad thing?'

Jess didn't smile. 'It usually is.'

Olivia picked up the book Jess had laid on the desk. The spine had a name embossed on it in silver letters: Catherine McLeod. 'Who's this?'

'Your granddaughter,' said Jess. 'She was born after your book was finished. Your son, Davie, she's his daughter.

Tears rose in Olivia's eyes. She suddenly remembered her Davie. He was a good looking boy, really clever at maths. She ached to hold him again, to smell his hair, to tell him she was proud of him. She closed her eyes and tried to picture him, married with kids of his own. Jess handed her a tissue.

'Oh, thank you lass, thank you for that news. I haven't thought about Davie for such a long time. This is his Catherine's book?'

'It is. But I have to warn you, reading it might not be a good idea.' Jess looked quite stern but Olivia was gripped by a desire to know. She took a deep breath and opened the book.

My life started with your death, she read. She could hear Catherine's voice reading her story. *I helped Dad to cope and that made me special. I would have been happy with that. I would have lived just fine with that little bit of special. Granddad made me more special, more special than anyone should be. Is it because you were not there? Is it your fault?* Catherine's voice faded away. Olivia dropped the book, heavily, on the table. Her breathing shook and tears started falling again.

'I don't understand,' she whispered. 'What am I reading?'

'This is Catherine's book and this section is a letter she wrote to you. Sometimes authors will write to those who have finished their books as a way of keeping their memories fresh or to simply get questions out of their heads. Once you write it down you can leave it behind and move on to the next chapter. I think that is what Catherine has done here.'

'What did he do?' Olivia asked fearfully. 'What did my man do?'

'I don't know,' Jess shook her head. 'I don't have permission to read Catherine's book.'

Olivia hesitated, then picked the book up again. She tried to open it at earlier chapters but the pages would not come apart. She could only read the same tiny paragraph over and over again. Jess suggested more tea, but Olivia barely registered her. 'What did he do?' she kept repeating. 'What did he do?' She felt sick and her face blushed in fear and anger. 'Why didn't anyone stop him?' Eventually she pleaded to Jess. 'Does anyone else know what went on? Anyone here? Can anyone read his book and just tell me what he did? I don't have to read it myself, I can just listen.'

'No,' Jess replied, firmly. 'He's restricted to us too. Until Catherine tells someone what he did and lets others into her book, he remains restricted.'

'I hope she doesn't,' Olivia stated. She knew it was selfish. She knew he should be confronted and made to answer for what he did. But where was Davie? Why did he not stop it? She knew a glimmer of understanding for Catherine's silence. There were no answers.

*

Olivia sipped her tea, unable to move, unable to think. 'When you've finished your tea I'll take you back to reception,' Jess smiled at her. Olivia nodded. She felt calm again. This cup of tea was just what she needed. She put the cup and saucer on the tray then stood up, put back on her coat and straightened her hat. Jess pressed the button for the lift and they waited in silence. The books were still being moved around and Olivia still couldn't see a pattern in what the librarians were doing. She turned to Jess, 'I've never seen anything like this before.'

'That,' said Jess, 'is what everyone says.'

Olivia clacked over the marble floor to the revolving door. She stepped out onto the busy street and tried to remember what she come to the Registry for. She was sure it was something to do with Mrs MacDonald, but she couldn't quite put her finger on it. Anyway, she had to get home because she was sure this was Tuesday and her magazine came on a Tuesday.

Three Microfictions
Robin Lindsay Wilson

SOMEWHERE IN BRITTANY—UTOPIA

The town was all drifting banners. The town was blue sky flutter. The town was hoisted flag. The town was waving red ribbons. The town was hanging with streamers from balconies and open windows. The town was dazzle white awnings. The town was celebration... The bunting was nothing to me. I had nothing to celebrate. I had a stern appointment in a bigger town. The town was a parade of prettified horses in my way. Rosettes in my way. Fireworks and smiles in my way... I abandoned my hired car. I abandoned my ETA and stepped into the festival. I heard my voice cheering with the crowd then becoming indistinguishable.

THEN AND NOW—UTOPIA

I never understood it at the time. Why an old couple would invite us to join them on their yacht for a sail. They took us out from Kristiansand on midsummer's day. The weather was perfect. High blue skies. We smiled the whole time the wind filled the massive white sail. We didn't have a care in the world. The old man did all the work. We sailed until the stars came out. Plunged past islands where bonfires were lit to celebrate the longest day. Sparks rose into the twilight. We couldn't stop laughing with the pleasure of it all. And that's all the old couple wanted. Nothing else. Just to share a little part of our youth. I understand it now. I'm sorry I haven't given them a thought in all this long while. I remember them now. I remember those bright young things in Kristiansand... If I had a boat today I would invite them on board.

RELIEF—DYSTOPIA

I found some sticks. They are big enough. We could put a plastic cover over. The people over there on the plain have got plastic. They have been here the longest. But we have only been here three days. The camp has run out of plastic. We have a little rice from the trucks. There is just enough for the children. I can walk to the water pipe. A mile is nothing when the water is clean and good. I have a plastic container. It has a red lid that snaps shut. I am happy with this container. I am happy the flood did not kill us. We are safe in this camp. If only we had a plastic sheet to cover our heads from the rain we would have everything. Perhaps tomorrow the plastic will be given.

Eaters of Dreams
George Lea

At last, *an end*. To stars, to light. To dreams. And in the dark after? A nightmare child, *our* child; spawn of dead suns, black-hole maggot, swelling in the wounds of God, after all between Heaven and Hell is done.

They come, my carrion-children, my fly-born, singing desolate lullabies, curdled hymns, in welcome of creation's leprosy.

Unwanted waking, my only prayer to sleep forever; that they never hear my dreaming lament. *Denied.* The Eaters of Dreams sing to me, call me *Father*, in the dark, despairing hours.

Worms call, black-hole dawn, gasping in the light of dead stars, my first breath, choked with dead Mother's filth, my own. A son of leprous Gods, my nightmares, new gospels that all waking and dreaming will soon know.

No prayers, now, save in cockroach tongue. Our Vermin Children come! Sing, my unwanted, my aborted! Sing and call them to cannibal feast.

Listen... the elegies of worlds, diseased stars. Beautiful, isn't it? No use praying now, sweet ones. Fairy time is over. Come! Come and join our choir...

Awake, at last; almost born. All know, the dreaming in their cribs, all see. Wailing in welcome, hearts stopping as one.

Don't mourn me; my dreams are over. Save your tears for when the black suns rise, when my nightmares are born.

Many, child; no dream survives, no garden is eternal. Let them show you the night beyond Eden.

The Same Place As The Last
Nina Anana

'Two, four, six eight, we don't want to integrate. Two, four, six eight, we don't want to integrate.'

Cecily stood off to the side of the partition to watch the march with her friends, having travelled from their muster point in Islington down to Parliament Square. The road adjacent to the march had been cordoned, with a barrier of police and security personnel standing guard. It was a grey autumn and if you had been away from the country for a fortnight, you might not have been privy to the change in government the night before. On a Saturday evening, crowds of tourists dominated the Central London rush.

The city had become a mausoleum to wayward ideas of English life, replete with pastoral recreations and empty signifiers. Its speed did not slow in the tide that had swept the country. After twelve years of turbulent opposition, the Worker's Democratic Empowerment Party had seized government. Cecily was proud to have played her part, having deferred her university revision under the guise of illness to join local party members canvassing. She watched the march as one would a spectacle; all that had existed in the tensions of different layers of society, reduced to representation.

The Stricters were marching again, shouting expletives and rhyming couplets in one breath, in what Cecily hoped was the swansong of a political current that had drowned the country for over a decade. She was twenty-three and completing her Masters degree; she never believed she would be among a crowd of counter-protestors pushing the Stricters back from the prominence and platforms they had come to possess in the media. The unit passing adjacent to her performed coordinated Nazi salutes to match the drumbeat of the chant: 'Two, four, six, eight. We don't want to integrate.' A nascent political scientist, Cecily sighed, for once unfazed by the sublimated violence.

Likely, only two among them understood the pedigree of the different refrains they had stitched into a chimera.

'What do we want? Unity.'

'When do we want it? Now.'

The chant had switched to another borrowed artefact. These were men fighting for homogeneity, to restore the halcyon days of the 1990s—although this was a tight point of contention. Fights had broken out in previous rallies, as those who wished the 1980s to be the reference point fought the former group, whom they considered progressive infiltrators. But one thing they agreed: society had spiralled into chaos once the Y2K clock had turned and not one computer that mattered was reset to zero—not even the ones recording their student loan debt and mortgages.

'Goodness, look at these monkeys,' a man standing beside Cecily uttered in a nondescript southern English working class accent. The barely veiled disgust struck her with a sense of alarm. 'They think this is all a show.'

'In a way it is,' Cecily replied, surprising herself; first, for speaking to a stranger, and second for the bluntness of her statement. The man looked her over carefully, squinting as if trying to piece together a broken frame. He opened his mouth, but decided against speaking. Cecily could see him conversing with companions, pointing in her direction as they nodded cautiously and inched away, deeper into the crowd.

In truth, she was disappointed by the tameness. The ire and retribution owed was eviscerated by the need to orchestrate the demonstration so far in advance. It was only permitted by the police within the one-month parameter for protests of that size in the city. Simon Robinson of the Stricters Britain Liberation Party showed up at the Shoreditch branch of police on the same day as Simon Einhorn of Workers' Democratic Empowerment Party, or so rumours had it. The friendly chatter between the men flitted from the weather to half-term holiday. Simon's daughter had started school, but he was afraid she would lose her English as the demography of the area had shifted from that of his days. Simon reassured him that it wasn't so bad; people needed to prove their knowledge of English to enter the country, after all. Besides, it was good to be bilingual.

'No, but not with those savage languages,' Simon replied, with a definitive middle class North London accent that caused them to look at each other with an air of mutual deference. They were not so dissimilar, Simon and Simon. Simon doffed his cap. It was the one he'd worn during his Trotskyist youth, an affiliation he liked to recall to comrades when they called him a Nazi for founding the Stricters. Simon nodded civilly.

'We will win,' Simon muttered under his breath as he left the office.

In the lead up to polling day, a frenzy had broken across the country. The stripped body of a girl was found, mutilated on the corner of Westminster and St. James. It was one in a series of violent acts, culminating in the slaying of a Workers Empowerment Party MP in broad daylight. The girl had been cut with hundreds of gashes by a sharp thin blade and her long black hair, hacked off haphazardly from her bloodied skull. Her breasts had been cut off her chest, and sharp letters carved out the words 'Slut' 'Invader' 'Whore' down from her tan, gutted abdomen. In the last bout of indignity, her bright celadon headscarf adorned with magnolia, was thrown beside the body, covering a hand on which all the fingers had been removed at the knuckles.

The Stricters marched the next day in celebration, but were disbanded due to the lack of a permit. They were, however, able to complete five miles of their seven-mile march before being intercepted by reluctant but perturbed armed police. They held up a poster with an image of the slain girl's body, circulated on Twitter, showing the words 'WE WILL NOT BE REPLACED.' Over the image of the girl's gutted womb, they had written 'DEPORTED' in bold red letters.

Cecily watched the spectacle, turning to her boyfriend Kwame in disbelief as the camera on the CBB channel panned the images held up at the march.

'Have we as a nation reached a breaking point?' asked a woman's disembodied voice from the television. 'Tonight, the CBB takes you behind the scenes and speaks to members of the Stricters to find out their demands.'

'Oh for godsakes!' Kwame exclaimed. 'How many interviews do these dickheads need?'

'I cannot believe this is their take so soon after this... event. What was her name, even? Do you know?'

'No, I don't think it's been published.' Dani was transfixed by her laptop, which cast an eerie mantle on her pale skin and dark blue eyes. An aspiring journalist, she had been following the story closely since it broke the night before. She had even gotten as far as ten feet to where the body had been removed, trying to gather what clues remained of the execution. Her attempts were aborted by the forensic clean up group, who washed the streets with a surgical attention to detail before removing the cordons. It was a busy intersection whose extended blockage had boded poorly for the tourist season, just then reaching its crescendo.

'Do we even know where she's from?' Kwame asked.

'She was probably Asahkih. Hard to tell. God it was awful.' Cecily sighed.

'I guess it's a bit moot now. What's done is done,' Dani said with a dejected resolve.

'I don't think it is, though,' Kwame replied. 'If she's Asahkih, she's likely one of the few that made the quota. Her family's likely dead already. We ought to do something.'

'Like what, protest?' Cecily asked flatly. 'By the time we get a permit the issue-attention cycle would have passed.'

'Guys, guys, must we talk about this ahead of the game? Goodness sakes, it's the weekend,' Dani reminded them, emptying a glass of Tignanello into her mouth.

'Ack, whatever. She's right. Telly off,' Cecily chimed, leaning in to grab the last of her friend's wine. 'You lush,' she pronounced in mock indignation as she finished the glass.

'Hey, hey, Kwame Kwam Kwam. My man!' a voice slurred, Someone stumbled into the flat Cecily shared with Dani. It was

John and Imogen; Cecily looked down at her phone, perturbed. John was already working on a can of Kronenbourg, which he held tightly like a precious jewel. Imogen's black hair was pulled into a severe bun, and she looked about hurriedly, eyes sunken and red from three consecutive fourteen-hour workdays.

'I'm so sorry Ces. I got out early today, but this oaf wouldn't leave the flat for forty minutes, waiting on a bloody delivery. How are you darling?' Imogen's Parliamentary Reporter internship was two months in, and she had already started to morph before Cecily's eyes. Cecily smiled tightly as she hugged them in turn, awaiting when she could ask Imogen about her week's encounters with members of the Cabinet.

'I'm alright, don't worry about it. You're on time. Not a minute too soon,' Cecily fumbled clumsily as Kwame walked back towards the living room, grabbing pistachios from the glass bowl in the corridor.

'For the record, the delivery was my Asahkih sponsorship card, which I had to activate online. Signed-for delivery, is anyone going to hold that against me?' John asked, spreading his arms in mock bashfulness as he took another gulp of Kronenbourg, finishing the drink and crushing the can before tossing it into the kitchen opening.

'John, stop littering!' Imogen screamed.

Kwame poked his head out from the front room.

'I'm indoors for god sakes,' John retorted.

'It doesn't matter. You do this all the time. You're killing the bloody environment.'

John scowled at his girlfriend, throwing an arm around Kwame as he joined the latter in the living room.

'Best of three poker tonight?'

'Sure thing,' Kwame toasted.

Sirens rang, three floors down on the main road, as they sat around the antique painted white coffee table Dani had borrowed from her parents. As they dealt the cards and downed wine, Cecily couldn't shake the steady sense of dread that had been building since she arrived home that evening. The busy high street that their flat block overlooked had settled with a calm that felt forced for a Friday night. Across the street, the evening news blared loudly from the television screen of a serious pub, the sort corporate types settled into after work to avoid the trappings of family life. Her eyes kept darting outside and across the street, as if waiting for someone to arrive.

'Fold,' Dani sulked, reaching for another glass after her last community river card was dealt.

'We've barely started!' Kwame looked over confused.

'I've got four fours, Kwame. All the ones in the deck. You can guess what my fifth card is.'

'That's a good fucking hand, are you serious?' John replied

'Oh,' Dani laughed. 'Never mind. Can I unfold? I've never played Texas Hold'em.'

'No second chances. You had plenty of time to learn the rules.' John was now more determined to make the most of his low-ranked cards.

'Bit harsh,' Imogen chimed.

'Doesn't matter. Everyone plays by the same rules or the whole system falls apart.'

'It's okay guys, I can hop in on the next round, or whatever.'

'No, that's rubbish,' protested Imogen. 'What kind of world do we live in, where people are not given a chance to right a genuine mistake? Can we seriously take a system that punishes the innocent so harshly?'

'Immy, please don't do this.' John looked over at his girlfriend. 'It's not about any one person. It's about upholding the rules of the game so everyone gets a fair chance.'

'But what if the rules are complicated, or unfair even? Don't people at least get a chance to learn them?'

Kwame looked back and forth between his friends, confused as to which portion of the discussion he had missed.

'Let's take a vote, because we really need to move on?' Cecily intervened.

'No way. The rules are right there, you don't get to vote on who cheats them, right, Kwame?' John looked over for support.

'Ah, guys, let's keep it moving. This round is taking a little long.' Kwame excused himself to grab another beer, looking out the kitchen window to take in the display of lights produced by a fleet of police cars gathered on the street below. He thought little of it; persistent sirens had become commonplace. He folded last that round, and John leaned in eagerly to note his victory, one more win to take the pot of £5000.00.

Cecily's hands shot up, joining the cheer as the newly elected Prime Minister made his way calmly onto the stage, in an unprecedented first public address. There was speculation that he wouldn't show up at the march that day, having been up into the late hours of the morning well after the votes had been called in his favour. John Stimson's balding white hair hung like a sweaty veil around his congenial, friendly face. His baggy, ill-fitted grey suit was like the borrowed fancy dress of one playing at Prime Minister, but at nearly seventy-five, he moved with the energy and verve of one decades his junior, and an earnestness that had cut through the cultural divide, galvanising disparate demographics from seats that were traditionally safe for the opposition.

Kwame made his way through the crowd, looking for Cecily; now that fascists and the resistance shared a parade, and it was a tight rope walk to find his way through to the right side of the shadows as dusk settled over the bleak grey skies. The Stricters' chants were soon drowned out by the rising applause as John Stimson approached the podium on the makeshift stage.

'Rise like lions after slumber, for they can never again vanquish so great a number!' he opened, in a poetic lilt that became familiar during the course of his electoral campaign.

'Yes, Mr. Stimson, we have waited, weak and alone,' a disabled man in a wheelchair shouted from the front row, and the crowd redoubled in refrain. Kwame squinted, finally spotting Cecily's bright red hair and green backpack next to the entrance of the tube station, five rows from the front of the stage. He wanted to seize her into his arms, happy that she was safe. Across the parliament green, unrest had broken out between the Stricters and a contingent of anarchists who called themselves the Lions of Freedom. He had hoped that Cecily and her friends were nowhere near this crowd.

'No more do you have to fear your freedom,' John Stimson continued. 'We have fought and won; the right heirs of glory, dipped in hope and a future that celebrates the abundance of this great nation.'

'Mister Stimson, what about the border people?' someone shouted from the crowd. Cecily looked around, cross at the attempt to dampen this hard-won moment. Damn journalists, she thought, probably from The Sentinel.

'We will take care of all. Everyone will know for the first time, what it is to be safe and thrive in a country that does not put a price on the head of humanity.'

This last statement hit a spot in the crowd, which rippled out in a gargantuan ebb, right to the periphery where Kwame stood, listening intently with apprehension.

'And let us not take blame for what has been done to the countless millions, who now flee their flooding homes to the last safe havens on our coasts, but we will do our best to make sure that they too do not perish because of the error of our predecessors.

'We will feed the hungry.

'We will enrich the barren.

'We will sate the thirsty and take care of what is left of this here, our wonderful planet.'

'But how, Mr. Stimson? The average person can barely afford to live. How do we ensure the safety of the border people in those dreadful camps?'

It was the same woman's voice, and now, a sense of unrest had replaced the convivial merriments. Whispers shot across the crowd like a dagger searching for its target. A security detail, hidden by plain clothes, dropped their cover and dove in towards the interlocutor. The whispers grew into a rumble as five guards latched onto her and dragged her towards the back of the crowd; she knew better than to resist.

'Gentlemen, let her go. You heard me, I said let her go,' John Stimson's voice boomed into the microphone. Nobody said we had an easy journey ahead… but hope is what we now have.' The woman was taken to the stage, 'What is your name, young lady?'

'Aoife,' she replied, trembling.

'Well, Aoife, I like your spirit. You are precisely the sort of person we need now to move our society forward. To ask the tough questions to which there are no easy answers. We need to empower the Aoifes of this world. We need to give a voice, where none existed. We need to rise up, and meet our new challenge with aplomb because today, we shake our chains and turn a new chapter. One of Love. One of Hope. One of Unity.'

A cheer rose from the crowd as John Stimson's voice waned. His speech went on in much the same way for nearly thirty minutes. Cecily and her friends refraining on cue, until their throats dried. Kwame looked out at the crowd quietly. He recognised the promises in John Stimson's speech; they were mere platitudes that blended into a well-composed, Prime Minsterly recitation. The evening's jubilations and verve sublimated an uneasiness, as the dispersed remnants of fascists littered the periphery, outnumbered, on this occasion.

The poker game was just what was needed to take their minds off the dreadful news. Across the pond, Texas had secured a referendum victory for secession, and against federal approval, had formed a convenient alliance with North Mexico, preparing to defend its borders. There was news of yet another ship off the Strait of Juan de Fuca, filled with residents of the islands of the southern coast of the Pacific Ocean. They had sailed two weeks to find a home in either Canada or America after the floods. Military was deployed to drown the ship, and execute survivors before they reached the shores. In the news, a woman with short, neatly coiffed blond hair read slowly:

'Invaders from The Solomon Islands and Tuvalu were today neutralised, trying to enter the country through the Strait of Juan de Fuca. On board, it was believed the invaders were failed asylum seekers who attempted to bypass the laws and rules of the country. The government has deployed a new strategy to track and stop those attempting to enter the country illegally, as the number of invaders continues to grow.

'Stay tuned, for an update on the winners of last night's Strictly Come Dancing.'

Kwame had watched Cecily strain against the blaring news from the pub below, knowing she had stayed her nerves in front of her friends with threadbare equanimity. He'd had enough of the news that night, as John skirted around the poker rules, locking them in tight and readying for a win. It was no way for a society to be. They were an hour into their game, before the guttural shouts started from blocks adjacent to their flat. At first it was a woman's shout.

'Leave Malthe alone, he was born here,' she said in perfect English. 'Stop it!'

The cries outside would have gone unnoticed, but for a fire burning steadily in the far corner of the quadrangle that formed the development's courtyard. Kwame had been grabbing another beer when he noticed the growing inferno, which drew little attention from the passers-by on the streets. From the fire, his eyes moved to the flashing lights of police cars, who were seven in all now.

'What's going on out there?' Imogen asked hazily as she swayed into the kitchen, topping up on wine and cashews.

'No idea, I think there's something burning out in the quad,' Kwame replied

'Move, let me see. Oh shit!' Imogen exclaimed, dropping her wine glass, a commotion that brought the rest of the flat's occupants into the room.

'What's going on?' Cecily cried as she took account of the shards scattered on the cream and black tiles of her kitchen floor.

'Immy, what the fuck?' John replied, bending to pick up the glass before he cut his palm and index finger with a large piece. The blood darkened the pool of wine on the floor as the rest looked on in horror.

'It's a raid,' Imogen shouted. 'John, are you okay? We have to go?'

'Go where? Ack, fuck,' John winced, fumbling for the nearby kitchen towel.

'There's a raid. Look.'

They clustered around the window, staring at the chaos through variegated lenses, which made it difficult to piece the scene into a coherent whole.

'Stop panicking, it's just some old biddy shouting at her child,' John grumbled

'John, don't be a prick for once, yeah?' Imogen replied. 'Look over there, there are people, children across the grass being marched.'

Cecily, Kwame and Dani pressed their faces against the windows of the lit kitchen, watching the procession carefully. More people emerged from the open door in the flat block between theirs and the corner fire.

'Maybe it's a drill. I think something's burning over there.' Kwame pointed, but no one else seemed to pay attention.

'They're taking them away, we have to go,' Imogen shouted, jumping as she grabbed her coat and ran down the five flight of stairs to where the police cars were parked.

'Juq. Juq, stay to the sides,' a girl's voice called out.

'Ama, don't shout at him,' a man could be heard saying as they joined the growing queue of extracted residents. From the looks of it, Juq was a boy of no more than ten, with tanned skin and pale green eyes that shot around, taking stock of his neighbours who'd been drawn out of their home in various states of dress. Mrs. Hajun was still wearing her grey house robe, holding a chipped mug with what must now be cold tea. She looked as confused as the young boy, who held tightly to a strip comic, still clutching to his bookmark as he walked over to join his parents. His bewildered expression caught Kwame by surprise, as he realised what must have been taking place. It was a neutralisation operation. He knew what would happen next, as the residents were marched onto the waiting white vans to undergo what the officials called a 'passport check'. From the look on the boy's mother's face, Kwame could tell that neither would pass the check. Imogen stumbled, unable to find footing as she watched the naïve residents queue obediently, believing that all they had to do was follow the law. But such pretensions had long since fallen by the wayside, with groups who had been peacefully settled in the UK rounded up in the dead of night. At times entire neighbourhoods went missing, as the government expanded their unending crusade to demonstrate toughness on immigration. There were only realistically two news channels now, with other outfits spewing mild variations on the same theme, and both had decided as a matter of mandate, not to discuss the disappearances, except for when one of the minor presses made enough noise to highlight the scandal. But the issue-attention cycle being what it was, such scandals faded into the background, overshadowed by a slaying or a fascist march and their attendant demands.

Ama, the little girl, who looked about thirteen years of age, trailed reluctantly behind them, holding a bundle of crumpled papers Kwame couldn't make out. Being older than the boy, she seemed more aware of their fate and only stared straight ahead towards where her parents were standing, waiting for their turn to make a plea.

'What's going on here, then?' Imogen asked impatiently as she approached one of the police officers near the check-in van. He was dressed in a green armoured vest and other hard-surfaced paraphernalia entirely out of place on their high street tower block. He looked her over vacantly, taking in her diminutive frame, before once again turning silently to face the approaching crowd.

'Hey, I'm talking to you. What law are you taking them under?' I'm a journalist, I will report this. What is your name?'

'Immy, for god sakes, shut up,' John groaned, tugging his girlfriend's arms. 'Let's get out of here, it's not your business.'

'Like hell it isn't my business,' Imogen fired, feeling more sober than she would have liked in that moment. 'Do you even know what they do to people removed like this?'

'Of course I know. But they broke the rules and shouldn't be here, Immy. Don't get yourself hurt, that guy doesn't look like he's playing.'

'Oh God John, you just don't get it, do you?' Imogen ran towards the centre of the procession, grabbing the recorder she kept on her at all times. John and Cecily followed closely.

'What are we going to do?' Cecily asked, running her hand through her hair repeatedly, until a few strands around the crown snapped. It was a bad habit she had picked up lately, and small but discrete patches were starting to show through her thick red hair.

'Stay calm, we're going to interview as many people as we can, start with the older children. You got a pen, Ces?'

'Uhh, no. I mean… just a minute, let me check. I can borrow one across the street.'

'Get some paper, too. We need as much of a record as possible.'

John looked on, bewildered by Imogen and Cecily.

'Look, Immy, there are legal ways to do this. Don't think I don't care, I pay £300 a month to sponsor these Ashakihs. And others who go through the right programmes. I have nothing to be ashamed for.'

'That's not the point, though, is it?' Imogen hissed. 'Your programmes allow about forty residents in a year, out of about ten thousand. Where do the rest go?'

'They're not residents, they're migrants.'

'Migrant would suggest they had a choice. One-quarter of the coast is under water now, John. Don't you see how this could be us someday, or if not us, our children? They had lives in their countries until the waters started rising.'

'I know that, Immy, but it's just not for us to interfere with the laws now. There are programmes that…'

'I'm not interested in your bloody lotteries!' Imogen shouted, breaking rank as she ran towards the group. 'Everybody listen. I need you to state your name, date of birth, country of origin, date of arrival. And let me know what papers you hold. We can help,' she gestured to Cecily, who had returned with a notebook and pen, shakily joining her friend just shy of the police cordon that was swallowing up the procession. The crowd paused and the mumbling died down, as eyes regarded her with tempered curiosity and fear. Nobody made a move towards her as the officer who had ignored her earlier readied himself at attention, speaking into his radio excitedly.

Kwame stood towards the edge of the scene with an acute dread, regarding the fire that had grown larger and was now licking the corner of the first floor brick walls. He walked closer, surprised that no one was taking stock of the growing inferno metres from where the crowd had been cordoned towards the spread of white vans. Imogen raised her voice with an authority she had honed reporting on breaking news. She projected through the crowd of frightened residents, until one broke through the queue. It was the little boy, Juq, who first approached Imogen, pointing to his parents and sister as he gave his vitals. Imogen knelt to hear his story, as his sister Ama ran towards him with wide hazel eyes, again showering admonishment on the boy. Kwame paused near to where Juq and his sister stood, and knelt along with Imogen, smiling to ease Ama's trembling hands.

'Don't worry, we won't let you go anywhere,' Imogen reassured. 'When did you come here?'

'I was the only one when my parents came over. He was born here,' the girl replied.

'Fantastic, do you have any other relatives here, someone who can vouch for you? Where are your parents?'

The girl pointed to where a slender woman with long black locks stood watching attentively. She too left the queue to join her children, where she was able to fill Imogen and Kwame in on the home they had left behind, in the now-flooded island country on the Pacific coast. She turned to beckon to her husband, and as they moved, others followed suit and make their way to where the three of them stood.

Kwame funnelled the crowed towards an orderly queue in front of either Cecily or Imogen for an interview. At this point, a few spectators appeared behind the iron-barred windows and barricaded balconies overlooking the tower block quadrangle to watch the chaos below, as Imogen and Cecily took information and directed calls for assistance. Kwame wiped sweat dripping from his brows, his deep brown skin glistening against the glow of the courtyard fire.

'Is anyone going to do something about that fire?' Kwame asked Cecily, who for the first time turned her attention to the closed off wall at the far end of the courtyard. Just then, he felt hands on his shoulder tugging with a grip intent on paralysis. Two police officers in padded vests and riot helmets pulled him from where he had been perched, shouting muffled commands he couldn't piece together. Two more joined them, as they threw Kwame to the ground and knelt on his back. Cecily shouted and ran towards him, but two more officers intercepted her and blocked her view, coaxing her to return to where she had been standing with Imogen. She and Imogen were then escorted off the green to a corner near the courtyard opening, where they were questioned about their evening's activities and interference. Imogen could hear John and Dani shouting as they attempted to bypass the police officers.

Kwame squirmed, confused for a moment about where he was, as a sharp pain shot from one side of his ear to the other. He looked up briefly to see the little boy Juq and his father shoved into one van while the little girl Ama and her mother were put in another. One by one, the residents were pushed back into the queue and slowly swallowed by vans before any other interference.

Kwame recalled this pain in his spine, the police man standing on his back, as he quietly watched John Stimson fan the flames of hope; he couldn't shake his reservations. Without being aware, he had inched closer to Cecily, ashamed at his own paralysis as he assessed the anonymous faces fast approaching them; pale, nondescript and partly covered. The infiltrators had moved into the ranks as a loud bang went up into the crisp evening air, followed by a cloud of yellow smoke. Cecily grabbed Kwame firmly. She looked around as people started to shift to both side of the square.

'What was that?' Imogen asked, grabbing Cecily's rucksack and pulling her friend towards the pavement.

'England lives!' they heard shouted nearby to the entrance of the tube station.

'England lives, England for the English,' came a refrain. A renewed riot was fomenting; Cecily heard the crash of a bottle land nearby and jumped. Kwame ducked on instinct, he felt like lightening was striking twice, and his heart kicked into a rhythm that outpaced his thoughts. His breath came in short bursts and his legs weakened as he tried to maintain focus and navigate the parting crowd. He could stand his ground and fight. All of them at once, he thought to himself with crushing raw anger as his eyes narrowed on the culprits.

'Race traitor,' came a voice nearby, and there, Cecily saw with stark lucidity, three blond men, two her age, wearing dark coloured hoodies that partly hid weather-beaten faces. In that moment, she could see everything about them in the painful wash of the amber street lamps. There were four moles on the neck of the one standing closest; his thinly pressed lips underlined a glare; she stepped back for fear that his hate might stretch out to consume her. The flash of green was like lightening as the man hurled the beer bottle he'd been holding across the imagined Maginot line, uttering something inaudible.

'Kwame,' shouted Cecily, forgetting herself. The night's pandemonium rose into a crushing dissonance of chords, and all around him, Kwame could only hear drums.

'Is he alright, Juq? Hey, hey, steady now, just a sip.'

'Hold his head up so he doesn't choke, James. Don't rush, what's the hurry?' Juq replied.

'Where did you find him?'

'Out in the square.'

'Alone?'

'Yup.'

'Is he awake?'

'Mostly. He's mumbling to himself now.'

'What's with his throat? What did Ama say?'

'She ran an initial diagnostic on him; he's fine physically, just a few superficial scrapes. Amelia says we should let him lie in the pod for another day or two. Come away.'

No matter which direction he tilted his head, Kwame's vision remained blurred and distant. He had tried to sit up when his torso gave way and he fell again into the soft, cloud-like mattress he had been placed on. His mind wandered first to Cecily; Where was she? He still remembered the impact. He moved his head, trying to locate his girlfriend and friends, but it was difficult to see beyond the blaze of the razed streets, consuming the edifice of the square. He tried to cry out, but a pain rose from his throat, which recalled the time he had burned three of his fingers in a blue flame, trying to retrieve a toy from a fresh chimney fire. He tried to sit up again, panicked that something had happened to Cecily.

'Ex... excuse me,' he started with parched lips. 'Which hospital am I at?'

'Hospital?' came a young man's voice.

'Yes, was I brought here last night? Who are you?'

Juq looked on with despair, cautiously awaiting James's departure before approaching the patient's pod. His clothes were of a curious garment and colour, the sort no longer worn; they were suffocating, coarse and splayed with competing texts, likely those of the maker, Juq surmised. He was warned not to speak to the patient until Ama had given dispensation. The patient's speech, although English, was somewhat unfamiliar, and Juq had to spin it through the translation software to locate the version of English his interlocutor spoke.

*

'What is your name?' Juq asked.

'Kwame. Why?'

'Oh, no reason, we just have had you down as number seven for over a week. A legitimate name, mind. Some people opt for numbers; it's easier that way.'

Kwame looked confused. 'How many days?'

'You've been here for over half a Labasbuuc. In good care, of course. We have the very best facility here. James, Amelia and I have always wanted to take care of someone, even if they passed out after a night of Tog.'

'Tog, what? Look man, can I call my girlfriend, she got hurt last nig... Oh shit.' Kwame tried to sit up again but the pain was so severe, he thought his vision had cleared for just a moment, and he could make out the face that belonged to the voice standing next to him. But when he looked around, only washes of pale green, grays and amber formed his visual field, and dividing this, was the tall, tanned brown figure of his doctor.

Juq, never one to follow instructions, pulled up a chair next to his interlocutor, getting closer than advised, as he prepared another strong tea, sweetening the concoction passed down to him by his mothers and guardians, with two tablespoons of honey.

'It's for your joints, drink up. Hold your neck steady and I can help.'

'Who are you anyway?' Kwame asked, hesitant to take a sip of the pungent lukewarm liquid that the man held to his lips.

'Who, me? Oh I suppose that would matter, you're not from here. Call me Juq.'

'Juq.' Kwame repeated, straining his neck as he leaned to the side, trying to retrieve an errant memory.

'Hey, if I clear your eyes, promise you won't run before you're discharged?' Juq asked. 'Ama is still preparing your test results, and it would look really bad if I let a patient get hurt on my first solo.' He looked around anxiously to ensure his housemates had left.

'Promise,' Kwame said.

With that, Juq leaned in, typing a sequence of numbers on

his palm before reaching in to remove the soft silicon shells that had covered Kwame's cornea. He watched the latter's eyes water, as he shrunk against the light of the pod room.

Kwame looked around him in awe, which quickly turned to worry.

'Where am I?' he turned to ask Juq, feeling an odd sense of familiarity as he examined the young man standing in front of him. He was tall with dark angular features that met with a surprising degree of congruence. His jaws were squared but slim, with speckles of a black beard growing in patchy tufts. His green eyes danced around the room, as he took in his patient's reaction to the well-appointed room in which he had been absently resident for over a week. A large, amber orb hung from the high ceiling, lighting the space evenly in all directions.

'Oh yes, that is the solar dial. If you don't like it we can change it. In fact, now that you're up, we can change the rooms to whatever suits your fancy. I'm sure James and Amelia won't mind. We always accommodate our guests.'

'No, it's not that, but...'

'Nothing is permanent. It's all light and shadows distributed across a digital substrate. Here, try neo classical, if that's your taste.' Juq tapped out a pattern in the palm of his hand, which changed the furnishings in the room to opulent creams, rich navy and silver. The blue sectional sofa turned into a cream brass-studded, Queen Anne-footed chaise longue. And the glossy green Lucite rectangular coffee table converted into one with bevelled glass and gold leaf stems.

'Or do you prefer industrial? Oh, I know, Post-Modernist, eh? This one used to be popular.'

The large industrial tanned leather sofa was replaced by a tatty orange cushion, turned inside-out, with the white cotton stuffing hanging out at the side. The slab of birch, which served as a coffee table, was replaced by a small sofa, turned upside-down, legs in the air, and a decorative vase in the shape of a trash can, sat empty atop of the inverted sofa.

'No, no, not that one,' Kwame uttered, through his bout of shock.

Juq went through permutations of décor until he returned to the original, with the sun orb hovering imposingly over the sky-painted ceiling.

'H-how did you do that?' Kwame asked.

Juq appraised his guest again. 'You really aren't from around here, are you?' It's amazing, I have always wanted to meet a foreigner, you know, one who had not done a tour in our part of the world. Rumour is there are still a handful lurking around. Is this your first time in London, then?' Juq asked, fascinated by Kwame's unreconstructed demeanour.

'Been? I was born and raised in London.'

'Impossible,' Juq chuckled. 'No one is born in London. All the birthing houses are well over twenty miles away.'

Kwame regarded his host, afraid to say too much. If only he could get outside, but first he needed to know where he was. He thought he'd try to trick the good doctor into giving this information away without rousing suspicion.

'I mean, after I was born of course, my mother and father came to London and I grew up here.'

Juq stared quietly for a few minutes. 'Why just those two? And didn't you make the mandatory tour required by sixteen? Wait, how many languages do you speak naturally?'

'Just English. I learned a little bit of French in school, but I'm rubbish at foreign languages. A friend of mine speaks Xhosa.'

'Ah, Xhosa. Ndibuze kwanto.'

Kwame shook his head.

'Here, try this.' Putting a soft blue pod into Kwame's left ear, Juq repeated himself. 'Ask me anything.'

'Like what?'

'Ah, much better. So you speak no natural languages. Fascinating, fascinating.'

'I speak English, I'm talking to you right now.'

'Yes, but I was speaking Xhosa just now. English is the baseline, a kind of universal non-language, disorderly, and lacking entirely in pragmatics,' Juq laughed.

'I see. So tell me, is the London Eye still open at this time?'

'Ah, yes. Just across the embankment, it's open at all hours. I could take you there when you're healed.'

'Thank you.' Kwame smiled, getting his bearings. 'Do you think Amy would mind if I went out on the foyer, you know, just to get some fresh air?'

'You mean Ama. Hmm… no, we mustn't do that. James has gone for the night, preparing for Tog, but Amelia might be back soon. I could activate a breeze, however. It's nothing like the fresh London air, but it will have to do. I hope you can understand.'

'Yes, that's alright. Hospital policy, I guess.'

'No, not at all. This isn't a hospital, those are reserved for serious surgeries only. This is my home, and James's and Amelia's. Don't get me wrong, having you here is a delight, we all dream of taking up the duty of caring, but it doesn't come about often. All the houses are equipped with this care pod for that reason. Don't tell anyone, but mostly we all just sleep in there.' Juq chuckled.

'Oh. So, if you're not a doctor… I can just go then?'

'Well, I suppose. I mean, you wouldn't betray my goodwill like that, would you?' And for the first time, Kwame saw his host's wild eyes settled from flight, into a rather sombre gaze. The former lay quietly on the mattress, unable to move, even if he had wanted to bolt out of the serene quarters with its many changing façades.

To Kwame's relief, on the fourteenth day of his arrival, he was finally able to walk about, although unsteadily. His host, spurred by Kwame's curiosity, put few restrictions on his liberty. Juq took immense pleasure in seeing his own world through Kwame's eyes and would intentionally take him to remote quarters where visitors were seldom permitted, just to see his reaction. It was one day before Kwame's results were due, and Juq had done all he could to distract his guest from his multiple attempts to wander outside in the hopes of finding someone named Cecily, whom the former kept calling his girlfriend. Juq didn't understand the concept, or the fact that where Kwame was from, one was only possibly allowed to have one female as a friend. How oppressive, he thought, but in seeing Kwame's distress, decided not to push the issue any further.

Perhaps he could let his guest wander, in exchange for having the medical lenses implanted back into his eyes. It was assurance that should Kwame try to run, Juq could have his sight deactivated. That evening, as they sat down for dinner within the house, Juq mooted the proposition to Kwame and he calmly accepted without protest. Juq then took the opportunity to slip him the red bowl of tea, which was meant to be the last in a regime that formed around his convalescence. 'I wish you were well enough to attend Tog,' Jug said, as they stepped on to the porch for the first time. 'But Ama would never forgive me.'

'What's Tog?'

Juq looked over at him, blushing, not knowing how much he was meant to tell his interlocutor before his results. 'Don't worry about it, I never really attend anyway, there's too much drinking, and well, other stuff. Amelia's got a tale or two, if you really want to know what goes down. Anyway, we should be going.'

Kwame stepped out into London with a sensation he could only compare to a brain freeze. There was a pain as he took his first breath in the city where he had grown up. The atmosphere was different to the medical pod. He had spent the preceding week dancing around his intentions, as Juq contemplated defying Ama's orders and letting Kwame out. It was only a day before his results, so what risk could there be? Juq asked himself over and over, until the question no longer bore a mark. He had run out of novelties to show Kwame, who on his part had become more withdrawn. Juq took this for a sign of his failure as a host. They had walked almost a mile down St. James' square before Kwame spoke, asking Juq where they were. There was a large bronze statue enclosed by rows of glass, crystalline buildings. Between the buildings were spreads of well-manicured greenery, being tended by a group of seven men and women in celadon suits.

'They have government gardeners working even on a

Sunday?' Kwame asked.

'What-deners?' Juq asked, his curiosity again piqued.

'Those people over there.'

'Oh, them. I guess they're working, but what's so special about a Sunday? Everyone works when they can, to help keep the space clean. It doesn't require much. We have compressor drones for that. But the flowers… you see the way they are shaped and spaced out every three inches? That takes a bit more art.'

'So, they're volunteers?' Kwame asked.

'Hmm, I'm not quite sure I know what you mean. We're all volunteers in some capacity. Everyone does what they can; we live here.'

'Oh,' Kwame replied, still not understanding. His stomach grumbled and he reached into the pockets of his newly allotted trousers. He reckoned he would be stuck there for a while, and would need to start thinking about how to sustain himself. The shock of St. James's Park's remade landscape had not quite dissipated. The buildings were like water drops, made out of a hard material that wasn't quite glass. On them, were reflected all manner of colours and configurations through the day, similar to the technology Juq had shown him inside his home. But how did he afford to live in these parts? Just two miles to the south, was where Kwame's home in Elephant and Castle was meant to stand, but the discomfiture that had only just welled in his consciousness as a sense of barrenness and hunger, belied the deeper fear that he truly was nowhere.

'Who is that?' Kwame pointed, staying his hunger as the strikingly sharp and elegant features of the woman in the bronze statue caught his eye again amidst the sea of glass; she looked like an ethereal, waterborne goddess. Even in her neutral tones of bronze, Kwame discerned the afro hair and full lips and smooth supple eyes, reminiscent of his own. He had never seen anything like it in a popular square, let alone near the parliament building they were slowly approaching. To his relief, this had maintained its familiarity, with the gold spires and brick exterior, which stood in stark contradistinction to the clear droplet-styled buildings that populated the area for miles.

'That's Dawn Motumbe, the last Prime Minister of England.'

'Prime Minister?' Kwame marvelled. 'What happened to her?'

'Nothing, really. She lived until the ripe old age of one hundred and twenty-five. This statue was erected to honour her last act of parliament, abolishing the institution.'

'So what is that building?' Kwame asked, pointing to the Palace of Westminster.

'That is the town market. But enough questions, let's go in and get lunch. I'm famished, aren't you?'

They approached the grand building's doors, which had been gouged out and replaced by transparent gate. At the entrance stood two women, handing out what appeared to be a leaflet. Today's menu and offerings.

'I don't, I don't have any money,' Kwame uttered, embarrassed.

Juq smiled, getting confirmation of an idea so profound, he refused to believe it possible. Money, he thought. What an interesting concept. But in that moment, his marvel morphed into a sense of horror, as he recognised the gravity of Ama's caution. As if on cue, the latter messaged him through the chip implanted in his arm.

'Juq, where are you?'

'At home, of course?'

'You're at home?' Oh god, thank goodness. Where is the guest?'

'He's here too, why?'

'Are you with him?'

'Yes, of course I am,' Juq answered incredulously.

'Okay, listen carefully. You have to leave the room now, and remain in isolation until I get back. Get him back into the pod and seal it.'

'Wh-what? Why?'

'Listen Juq, really listen for once. We're in trouble. But if you've kept him in the house, it should be contained. No matter what you do, please tell me you won't let him out. Lock his vision please.'

'Ama, we are at home, but what has happened?'

'Just wait for my report. Act normal and don't let him know anything.'

Juq moved his thumb away from his arm; the signal cut off.

'It's okay, I can...I guess I can find a job?'

'No, no that's not it,' Juq looked over panicked. 'You're my guest, so you eat under my contribution. What do you want? Make it quick.'

Kwame hated charity and hesitated selecting from the opulent foods he couldn't quite discern. There was steak of some kind on a table of glass, but it wasn't from any animal he knew. The creams and buttered infusions were shades of purple and yellow, although he could sense from their fragrance a delicious concoction of the sort he could rarely afford. 'How much will this come to, I can pay you back?'

'Look, you sound like the The Invisible Hands when you talk like that, try not to mention money so loudly.'

This was a middle class affectation Kwame had never warmed to, the shame of talking about money, even as one desperately needed to know where they stood in relation to it.

'When can I pay you back?'

'Pay me back? Why would you... You'll get around to contribu...' Juq's voice trailed off. 'Money isn't required, only contributions.'

They walked through the stalls, picking up rich pies, gravies and meats tender and rich. Juq closed his eyes in a moment of appreciation as he took the first bite.

'Same as usual, Juq?' asked a middle-aged woman as they approached the fruit stand.

'As always, Emily. How's the garden?'

'Big this year. Everything came up on time, just as the season broke. We got a little more than anticipated, so Joshua, Bimi and I have been working four hours a day to get it harvested in time for market opening. Here, take a bite. And one for your friend.'

'Mmm. Definitely worth the toil,' Juq confirmed. 'Emily has

got the fruits down to an art, isn't that right?'

Emily blushed before launching into the details of the work she and the garden contributors had done to find the optimal strain, size and timing for the fruits.

'We are seven in all, now. I know it's not recommended that people contribute more than sixteen hours a week, but it's a large garden,' Emily huffed as she hurried to wrap up their fruits. 'You should stop by tonight, Juq; we have an open theatre on the veranda at sundown.'

'I'll try,' Juq answered, looking down. He was tempted by his favourite area of contribution, acting in improvised plays written by Emily and her old cohort, even as the need to get Kwame back to the house became more pressing.

'I didn't know you act?' Kwame beamed, beginning to feel at ease as they finished their late lunch. 'I used to run my uni drama club.'

'You could join in, the play is open to everyone,' Juq replied excitedly. 'This one only has a few open parts, so you learn your lines before curtains. Other nights allow improv.'

'Oh, I don't know, I haven't acted in a while. Don't you need professionals?'

'Professional actors?' Juq laughed. 'Why would you want to make a profession out of that? You contribute your acting. You would need to wait for the autumn's intake at the academy if you wanted to do it fulltime; they teach you a few things here and there. But tonight is just fun, the crowd will be small and the fire big. It's entertainment for the day's contributors before they head home for dinner. Emily's creations are great, tonight she's putting on an old favourite.'

'What's it about?' Kwame asked, lying against the soft green grass and gazing dreamily at the lavender sky; it was the filter applied during the post-lunch rest, and although discombobulated, he was slowly acclimating to the peculiarities of the London he found himself in.

'It's called Die Dreigroschenoper, re-mastered by our very own Emily. It tells a tale of a time so cruel, the very few hoarded all that was contributed to society, while the rest, by this very privation, were forced into penury. We know it wasn't quite so black and white, pardon the anachronism, but things got worse, before Dawn Motumbe was elected into office.'

'So what's fun about it?' Kwame asked, irritated by the scientific and detached way in which Juq spoke of a time that seemed mere days before: families hoarded onto white vans and exterminated; bread at ten pounds a loaf; rising insurgency as people looked for the weakest target on whom to punch down. This couldn't be London, he thought angrily. This was a practical joke, and he had better get looking for Cecily.

'Well, that's just it. It isn't funny, despite the comedic bent. There used to be a morality attached to allowing the few to hoard contributions, while not blaming anyone other than those who had even less,' Juq said incredulously. 'It was actually a spectacle of sorts, to centre and blame the poor. They were thought to be morally weak, and anything they did to survive was seen as a moral failure. Can you imagine reducing human beings to such a state when there was so much around to prevent such privations?'

'Yes, yes I can.' Kwame thought of Cecily in her soft pink floral dress. 'Yes I can,' he said again with a sordid ache that nearly erased his composure.

'And the violence. What was it that men were meant to prove in those days?'

'This sounds like a tragedy,' Kwame replied. 'What part would I play?'

'Umm, well, we don't have much time, uh… perhaps you could play the second beggar. You do know what beggars are, don't you?

'Yes, yes.'

'Well, you must be a very well-read man,' Juq patted him on the back.

The two men walked back, further east, taking in the scene of the undulating but constant architecture that characterised Juq's London. Kwame nodded, dizzy and uneasy. His guide again ducked into a corner, tapping on his palm as a chip lit up.

'Juq, where are you? Seriously, please tell me you're just in one of the conservatories on the perimeter of the house. We'll have to quarantine it, but no matter.'

'I'm in one of the conservatories on the perimeter,' Juq stated, his voice wavering.

'Don't lie!' Ama shouted. 'James has just combed through the house. I'm on my way.'

'Why do you need me there anyway, you said you'd call later to explain?'

'Not you, the man you are taking care of. He's septic.'

'Septic?'

'Yes, we've found strange incubated viruses in his blood, which have not been known for over a century. We have to contain him.'

'W—wait. What do you mean, viruses?'

'Juq, you need to listen to me. You have to get back to the house now. How long have you been out?' Ama asked frantically.

As the latter gave him instructions on how to quarantine himself, Juq looked over to his new friend.

'There's still an opening for Lucy Brown's character,' Juq informed Kwame. 'It's very short and should be easy to memorise quickly.'

'But that's a girl's role, right?'

'It's all acting. What of reality survives after a suspension of disbelief?' Juq asked.

They had travelled in personal pods across Central London, landing near the north, when Juq was met by a small group, which included five adults and three children. One of the women looked familiar, like Kwame had met her in another lifetime. She stepped forward and kissed him on the cheek, and then Juq. She had a gracious mound of black hair on her head, braided in intricate patterns along the side, with dark almond brown eye framed by thick black lashes. Kwame could not take his eyes off her, half out of intrigue, but also out of a sense of fleeting familiarity.

'Good to see you in these parts, Juq.' She embraced the latter, kissing him as well, but this time on the lips, as her hands slid down to his waist. Juq blushed, kissing her back.

'Just showing my friend around. I have him over at mine for convalescence.'

'Oh, you're caring, I'm so jealous.'

'This is Kwame, he's come from... the coast,' Juq said, patting Kwame on the back. It was then that he realised that Juq must have been on to his own suspicions. The whole landscape looked wrong, mislaid, like the inversion of a wayward dream. And yet...something of familiarity seeped out of the fissures.

'Evangeline, nice to meet you Kwame,' the young woman smiled. She made her rounds, introducing Kwame to her partners, her child, their father and surrogates respectively, and two children they were fostering until homing. 'This is Huy, Lily and Seun,' she pointed to the three children, who bowed politely, observing Kwame with piqued curiosity. In fact, it was the children's earnestness, which had recalled the stark contrast between where he was and the London he knew. It seemed that no one had stared at him in anyway that reminded him that he didn't belong, nor had they crossed the street on his approach, as he was ordinarily accustomed. He didn't have to worry about making himself less intimidating to people who believed his skin colour was enough to justify their fear. He smiled, realising that he had gone the whole day without thinking about such things, until he had been met with the children's curiosity.

'Hi, how do you do?' Kwame knelt to the children. The frightened expressions on their faces recalled the painful night in the courtyard, with the fire and vans. They looked just like the children who were being carted off with their parents to an end they could not anticipate.

'I'm well, sir,' Lily answered. 'Where are you from?'

'Lily!' her mother snapped. 'Mind your manners.'

'But I just wanted to know if he's from far away.'

Kwame smiled. Children and animals, they always knew. It wasn't just his clothing, half of which was now borrowed from Juq, but rather an essence about him, which despite his reticence, made its impression on those who assessed with few prejudices. It could go either way, Kwame thought. But here, they were taught kindness.

'I'm actually from London,' he replied, smiling at them.

'Then why are you speaking to us in Altish?' Lily asked.

She touched the switch of her translator, turning it off and listening to Kwame carefully. He too had been fitted with an ear bud and now, an activation chip, which allowed him to change between over five thousand languages and dialects translated in real time.

'That's enough, Lily,' Evangeline replied.

'Pardon us, Kwame, they're just grumpy from a day of 3-hour rehearsal. You see, the children are putting on their own play while we attend Tog. It happens every Labasbuuc.'

He wanted to ask what Tog was again, but stayed his curiosity when he remembered the look on Juq's face earlier.

'It was nice to meet you, Evangeline, and Chika, Tom, Grela, Sabir. And the children,' Kwame said, looking at the three with redoubled merriment.

'Will I see you tonight?' Evangeline asked, still holding on to Juq.

'Quite likely not. We're heading to Emily's play, and then… and then a few other things.'

'Don't stay away too long,' Evangeline cooed. 'It has nearly been a month since I last saw you.'

They were headed towards a diorama depicting a scene, not unlike the nativities Kwame knew from childhood. It was only partly concrete, with changing images projected onto it at different angles. Kwame was in awe of the richness of hue and artistic detail that went into what he considered a mundane scene. It was a depiction of a man, dishevelled and unkempt, sitting on a pavement with his jacket laid out in front of him. They drew closer and he could hear some indistinct chant; the coordination in their tone was unmistakable. It was a protest.

'Was that your girlfriend?' Kwame asked.

'Girlfriend? Juq laughed. 'You are strange. Evangeline is a partner; I take quite a fancy to her. She used to contribute as a history professor, now she's doing mechanical engineering. Her team helps maintain the personal pods and public pedways. Gorgeous, isn't she?'

'Yeah, she's alright. So you mean you two aren't a thing, because it looked pretty tight from where I'm standing.' Kwame nudged Juq.

'Oh we're many things. Lovers, companions, but most of all, exchangers of ideas. Evangeline has the strangest theories about human nature, and why we are innately compelled to take on the duty of care towards each other, especially those in a state of weakness. She's written philosophical papers on why human beings, in their natural raw state, are compelled to contribute as much as they can, just as we do today, and actualise their desires through the freedom that is an innate part of our will. Radical departures from this, she believes, is a form of perversion of human nature, born of privation and poverty.'

'Is that so?' Kwame smiled. 'So what happens if people are born poor, for example, and don't have the choice but to sell things… sell things they'd much rather not have to?'

'I don't understand. Why would they be born poor? Are the contributions withheld from them for some reason? Because even people in temporary restraint facilities are given the nutrition, social and emotional contact they require, while they contemplate their transgressions.'

'So everyone, is just given everything? Would that not make them lazy and not want to work?'

'Why would they have to work, per se? Contributions are based on talent, will and the training provided by the council. See, we are disposed to preoccupy ourselves, one way or the other. In fact, boredom is a symptom of a lack of will, or the opportunities to actualise a will. Whether you are good at doctoring, teaching, decorating, painting, entertaining, these are things that come together to make society whole. We are trained in multiple disciplines of our choosing, and most people go through six fields of contributions in their lives here. They give, where they are most talented, and the reward is society, constituted as it is. Anyway, Evangeline is better at these things than me. You should catch up with her sometime if you want to know more. She's a delight.'

'Two, Four, Six, Eight. Markets will not depreciate.' The protest was gathered at the entrance of the diorama, chanting as they paraded.

'Who are they?' Kwame asked.

Juq shrugged. 'The Invisible Hands. You see their brooches?'

Kwame scanned one of them, a young woman, and saw the bronze pin on her beige tunic, depicting a hand with its fingers splayed.

'What do they want?'

'Why don't you ask?' suggested Juq.

'Our list of demands are simple,' began an earnest young man, who looked into the middle distance as he spoke to Kwame, speaking without inflecting his voice. 'We want freedom to place an objective value on contributions, as well as the artefacts we amass by our contributions. This way, we could store it up, and trade our possessions for a currency, which would serve as a repository for value, for a latter date.'

After they had moved on from the strange man, Juq told Kwame, 'Most people see them as a nuisance. Why would we pay for the things we contribute towards bringing to being? And why restrict access to just those with a value repository, when there is plenty to go around? They come out once a Labasbuuc. It's the same thing, money this, money that. They believe in an invisible hand that will distribute the proceeds of contributions evenly, according to some innate logic. Have you ever heard of anything so absurd?'

'No,' Kwame replied, thinking back to his conversations with Cecily. Nausea had risen in his stomach, and he struggled to keep his balance as they stood in the queue to enter gates that opened to the diorama itself, even more specular up close. Kwame reached out to try and touch the digitally projected rain falling around the statue of the beggar, who held out what looked like a timepiece, with five others laid neatly on his jacket as the rain fell on them.

'Time for sale. That's what the Invisible Hands want,' Juq spat. This is from the old days. The design has changed, but the image is the same.'

And just like that, it clicked. Kwame panicked, looking around himself as the figure in the diorama moved, gesturing to him with the watch in a grotesque manner that evoked the uncanny valley. The people around him were like an image out of focus, even their strange flowing attire, which was worn by men and women, seemed to make sense. Kwame switched off his translator for the first time since arriving, and looked back at his friend. Asked him what time it was.

'Kloken uno. Whye the frage?' Juq replied. Kwame realised that he could not understand his friend at all. The dialect had so accelerated, it no longer bore a semblance to the English he spoke. He thought back to the little girl's question, and her mother's reticence. He looked at Juq anew, and his friend realised that Kwame had come to the same realisation as he had.

'What year is it?' Kwame asked, turning his translator back on.

'2135. Where are you really from?' Juq asked solemnly.

'Here, but then from a different...' His speech trailed off as his vision went blank. Wh—what just happened? Did you cut my sight? What did I do?'

'Oh shit, it wasn't me,' Juq replied in a panic. 'I thought we had more time.'

Just then, Ama's call came.

'Juq, I warned you. This is now an emergency.'

The crowd scattered as they received a message to clear the area. Everyone except the Invisible Hands, who remained firmly in their huddle, shouting about money. Children were evacuated first, as the adults took hold of the ones they could and dragged them outside of the perimeter of the falling digital veil.

'Don't say anything, just follow me, trust me.' Juq grabbed his friend's hand and they ran towards the foliage in a nearby park, just as the veil settled, capturing only the proselytising Invisible Hands.

'Where are we? What's happening?' Kwame asked.

'Your tests, they came back with results Ama didn't like. They want to contain you, but at this point they'll be looking for me too.

'What will happen?'

'I can't turn your sight back on at the moment, but just follow me, I'll get you somewhere safe. I'll tell you everything then.'

They rounded what Kwame assumed was a corner, and hopped onto a personal pod. Kwame's feeling of nausea had returned, and he fell over, as they exited the pod and ducked somewhere Juq had told him led to Evangeline's house.

They were met by two people dressed in protective clothing around their flowing suits.

'I wouldn't do that if I were you, Juq.' Through the mask, Juq could hear that it was Emily's voice. They had sent someone he trusted to carry out the negotiation. Kwame was expecting the police and a violent encounter, but Emily merely approached them, took Juq's hand, and they sat on the stairs.

'You know I hate deputising as a custodian, it's the least favourite of my contributions, but we can get this done quickly.' She looked over at Kwame. 'I'm so sorry Kwame. When you think of it, we're all in the same boat now. I too will be quarantined.'

'Where are you taking me?' Kwame asked. 'I won't go without my sight.'

'I'm so sorry, I'm afraid I can't restore that, not until you are treated; you will be fine soon, just a Labasbuuc in treatment,' Emily reassured. We can all go in together.'

But as she said this, Kwame jumped up and started running in a direction he couldn't see.

'Kwame, don't. Please wait,' Juq shouted, and would have run after his friend had Emily not put a hand on his shoulders.

'Don't go, he won't get far. He'll only be stopped by a barrier; all the sensors are on alert in the area so nothing will hit him.'

And with that, they heard a bang. Kwame had run into the erected barrier and had stumbled, falling back. Ama, Juq and Emily ran towards him to ensure he wasn't injured, just as a second barrier began to descend, a beeping sound warning all passers-by to clear the area.

Kwame felt a dull pain in his left shoulder. He shifted on his bed as he opened his eyes and his vision cleared. Some large machine was beeping at regular intervals and it started to overwhelm him as he struggled to regain composure.

'Oh thank goodness you're awake,' Cecily screamed, hovering over him with tears that soaked through the top of Kwame's hospital gown. He looked around at the large, clunky machines and physical tubes that fed into his arms, laying in silence.

'Where am I?'

'You… in hospital. You don't remember?'

He tried to focus, thinking back to the last time he saw Cecily's face.

'You hit your head. They found you out in the square. I was looking for you all night. Oh I can't believe it Kwame.'

'Kwame remembered the men with the hoods, their chants.

'Two, Four, Six, Eight…'

'Here, take a sip, hold your head up. It's for the pain, the nurses told me to give it to you when you woke,' Cecily said.

He remembered the look of pure hatred as they regarded Cecily and himself. He remembered jumping to cover Cecily as the projectile bottle flew towards them, but nothing else. He reached out to touch his neck, where a small, padded bandage was stuck. The injury wasn't as bad as he'd thought, but his head could not avoid the concrete wall of the tube station. His heart sank, as he realised that he was in London, back in his time, dreading another day of protests. He reached out and pulled Cecily into him, kissing her as she laid her head on his chest. The pain was sublimated by the feeling of safety, right then and there in that small hospital room. The television monitor in the room broadcasted a steady stream of news headlines.

Today, a shipping container was found with three-dozen invaders approaching the port. They have been sent in for rectification. Kwame reached for the remote and switched off the monitor. He blinked, feeling around on his body until he reached his face, where he felt small, barely visible pods, still tucked into his ears.

'Please, I cannot pay now, but I need to see him. We'll give everything we have,' a voice pleaded from the next room.

'Who is that?' Kwame asked, sitting up discombobulated. 'We should help her.'

'Help her with what, what is she saying?' Cecily asked, looking puzzled at Kwame.

'We need a translator quickly. Sir, do you speak Urdu?' a nurse asked Kwame.

'I... I think I do?' Kwame replied. The woman spoke again, and Kwame sat up, walking to her. But he could only reply in English. This was enough for her. She understood his reassurances and calmed down, as Kwame conveyed her concerns to the nurse.

Biographies

Nina Anana is a writer who hails from Canada. She has an interest in social satire, philosophy and Dostoyevsky, and is forever thinking of ways to bring these elements to life in novel form. When not writing, Nina enjoys exploring botanical gardens and other natural haunts in and around London.

Fiona Ashley is an English teacher and business owner, but always wanted to be a writer. She graduated from the University of Glasgow, MLitt Creative Writing (Merit), in 2009. She quickly had two short stories published in *Sushirexia* and *Invisible Ink*. Everything was going her way. Until it wasn't. Her delightfully complicated LGBTQ+ family needed me. She now returns to writing with certainty. She was recently selected to read from her work work at New Writing Showcase in Glasgow and her story, *Unidentified*, is to be published in the next edition of *From Glasgow to Saturn*.

Sonya Blanck is a pseudonym.

Rowan B. Fortune is a utopian obsessive living in the city of London, the home of utopians throughout history—from Thomas More to James Harrington and William Morris. He writes fiction and non-fiction on the subject of utopias as well as many other subjects, and does freelance editing for aspiring and established authors through Rowan Tree Editing.

Ben Jacob is a graduate of the University of East Anglia Creative Writing MA. He lives and works in Exeter, Devon. @benjamin_writer

George Lea is an unfixed oddity that has a tendency to float around the UK Midlands (his precise location and plain of operation is somewhat difficult to determine beyond that, though certain institutions are working on various ways of defining his movements). An isolated soul by nature, he tends to spend more time with books than with people, consumes stories in the manner a starving man might the scattered debris of an incongruously exploded pie factory, whilst also attempting to churn out his own species of mythological absurdity (it's cheaper than a therapist, less trouble than an exorcist and seems to have the effect of anchoring him in fixed form and state, at least for the moment). Proclaims to spend most of his time '…feeling like some extra-dimensional alien on safari,' which he very well might be (apprehension and autopsy will likely yield conclusive details). Following the publication of his first short story collection, *Strange Playgrounds*, is currently working in collusion with the entity known as 'Nick Hardy' on the project *Born in Blood*.

Greg Michaelson—I'm Edinburgh based, and I like to write about how things aren't and how they might be. My fiction, mostly short stories, has been published since 2001, in venues including *New Writing Scotland*, *Valve*, *Takahe*, *Firewords* and The Eildon Tree. My novel *The Wave Singer* (Argyll, 2008) was shortlisted for a Scottish Arts Council/Scottish Mortgage Trust First Book Award.

Jez Noond lives in Sherwood and teaches games design at a large city college in Nottingham. He enjoys photography and travel. In recent years, he has journeyed throughout Eastern Europe and into Russia. New places and the unfamiliar provide the impetus for writing. His short fictions have been anthologised in several Cinnamon Press publications. He is currently assembling a collection of stories and finishing a novel.

James Perrin is a mountaineer and travel writer. His short story collection, *A Snow Goose and other utopian fiction*s (from which his contribution to this collection is drawn) was published by Cinnamon Press in 2013.

Diana Powell has won the Allen Raine Award, and the Penfro Short Story Prize. In 2016, she was long-listed for the Sean

O'Faolain competition, short-listed for the Over-the-Edge, and was a runner-up in the Cinnamon Press Award. Her fiction has featured in a number of anthologies and journals. Her novella, 'Esther Bligh' has recently been published by Holland House Books. She is currently working on another novella, and a collection of her stories. She and her husband live in West Wales, and when she is not writing, she works in her woodland garden, or walks on the beautiful coast.

Omar Sabbagh is a widely published poet, writer and critic. His first collection and his fourth collection are, respectively: *My Only Ever Oedipal Complaint* and *To The Middle of Love* (Cinnamon, 2010/17). His 5th collection, *But It Was An Important Failure*, is forthcoming (Cinnamon, February 2020). His Beirut novella, Via *Negativa: A Parable of Exile*, was published with Liquorice Fish, March 2016; and he has published much short fiction, some of it prize-winning. His Dubai novella, *Minutes from the Miracle City*, is also forthcoming (Fairlight, July 2019); and a study of the oeuvre of Professor Fiona Sampson, *For the Love of Music*, will be released by Anthem Press in 2020. He has published scholarly essays on many 19th and 20th century writers, as well as on many contemporary poets. Many of these works are collated in, *To My Mind, Or, Kinbotes: Essays on Literature* (Whisk(e)y Tit, 2019). He now teaches at the American University in Dubai (AUD), where he is Associate Professor of English.

Robin Lindsay Wilson was born in Australia of Scottish parents. He now lives in Glasgow and works as a lecturer in acting and performance at Queen Margaret University, Edinburgh. He has had two collections of poetry published by Cinnamon Press—*Ready Made Bouquets* (2007) and *Myself and Other Strangers* (2015). His work has appeared in many UK literary journals and poetry magazines, including—*Iota*, *The Rialto*, *Brittle Star*, *North Words*, *Magma*, *The Interpreter's House*, *The Edinburgh Review*, *Dream Catcher*, The Journal, *Envoi* and *South*. Robin is currently working on his third collection of poetry.